WHEREVER IT IS SUMMER

WHEREVER IT IS SUMMER

TAMARA BACH

TRANSLATED BY SIOBHÁN PARKINSON

Little Island

WHEREVER IT IS SUMMER

First published in German in 2012 by Carlsen Verlag GmBH under the title *Was vom Sommer übrig ist*

This edition published in 2016 by

Little Island Books
7 Kenilworth Park
Dublin 6W
Ireland
www.littleisland.ie

Text © Carlsen Verlag GmBH 2012
Translation © Little Island Books 2016

The author has asserted her moral rights.

ISBN: 978-1-910411-56-8

A British Library Cataloguing in Publication record for this book is available from the British Library

Cover design by James Loughman
Typeset by Gráinne Clear

Printed in Poland by Drukarnia Skleniarz

Little Island is grateful for funding from the Goethe Institut for the translation of this book

Little Island receives financial assistance from The Arts Council (An Chomhairle Ealaíon)

The publisher acknowledges the financial assistance of
Ireland Literature Exchange (translation fund), Dublin, Ireland
www.irelandliterature.com
info@irelandliterature.com

10 9 8 7 6 5 4 3 2 1

(…) every summer
we want to get lost. Every autumn
they find us again. What a pity.

– Alexander Gumz, 'Instead of an Exit'

LAST CLASS

'Hey, look! We have a guest today,' he says. Accompanied by a smile, which is not right, because he can't stand Paul. But then he's leaving. Won't be putting in an appearance after the summer, hasn't shown up for the past two weeks, has his walking papers. And so there's something forgiving in his expression, and that's why he's calling him a 'guest'. Last day of school. Sit back. The last two classes are a form-teacher period. Paul sits back, sitting where he's sat for the whole year, there at the window, his arms on the window sill, with a view of the whole room, the outside world at his back.

I haven't swapped desks. That place beside Paul hasn't been mine for two months now.

'So what did you expect? Now that we won't be seeing each other any more? Some people won't be coming back after the holidays ...?'

The sun has been shining directly into the room since just before break, and it's warmed up. So let's sit back. It's too warm to sit up straight.

I'm not looking at him. I've had this blind spot for the

1

past two months, and he's sitting right in it, so I can't see him there at the window. I've been deaf in one ear for the past two months.

'And Lisa, what are you doing?'

Lisa answers something. Paul isn't asked. Everyone knows what Paul is doing. He's going to a school where you don't have to do maths. Everyone knows he's leaving the sinking ship, his court, his retinue. What's going to become of you?

'I was just thinking, you might have had a little something planned for today ...' says himself there at the front. There are always three dots at the end of his sentences, as if there is something missing, fill in the gaps.

No, sir, nobody has dreamt up anything for today. Nobody's got a song to sing, no-one's brought a story. Maybe he's expecting us to give him a present, something to say he hasn't totally wasted the last two years with us, some kind of a book with pictures maybe, or, better still, something handmade, something everyone helped to make. Nothing. Just three dots and 28 degrees Celsius in the shade by 11.15.

Having a thick skin doesn't make the heat any easier. When I lean forward, just to change my position, that spot by the window comes into view and I can see an elbow and a blue eye looking at me, and nobody sees how he's looking, and at the same time he's talking to the girl beside him, the one who took over my place at some stage. He only looks at me briefly, and there's nothing there, only coldness, which isn't a problem, considering how hot it is. Nothing matters any more, now that there's only thirty-eight minutes left of the school year.

TO DO

- Find a job (Corner Bakery?)
- Pick up Bonnie from Gran's
- Ring the driving school
- Mend bicycle tyre
- Clean up school shit
- And holidays – or something of that sort

BACKGROUND – OFFICIAL VERSION

My parents say it's a piece of luck that my mother (who is a nurse) and my father (who's an electrician/handyman) found work at the same hospital, which they've both been able to hang onto for years, because: only people who work and toe the line don't get fired when there's a rationalisation. And what a stroke of luck to have found a little house only five minutes from the hospital, the way the child (that's me) can always be near her parents. I mean, a house! Not a flat! With a garden!

My parents say it's all down to planning, that the child (me) is minded, that the house is kept shipshape, that everything goes smoothly, and nothing gets out of control.

My parents work shifts. My parents are at home in shifts. At home, there's a father shift and a mother shift. There are brief periods when they are both at home, and they are at pains to ensure that one of them is always awake.

My parents say it's very quiet here, and so green, and work is so close, and it only takes the child (me, Louise Helene Waldmann) a quarter of an hour to get to school by bike. And besides, there's a bus every quarter of an hour, in the evening as well, and every ten minutes at peak times. That it's no problem for the child (me, yes, me) to go into town occasionally on her own, or even to go out in the evening. At that age, you can't be soooo protective of the child (me-me-me-me), you have to loosen the apron strings a bit, don't you? My parents aren't a bit like that. My parents let the child (me, for Christ's sake, me) out! And they don't have to enforce the waking shifts and the rules about being always there the way they used to have to do when the child had just started at secondary school, when you had to be worrying if she'd manage it at all, especially when the parents (my parents) hadn't finished secondary themselves. And the child was taken aside and told that they wouldn't be able to help the child beyond a certain point, and the child had nodded bravely. And the parents had managed all the same, for years, to make sure the child got a hot meal at lunchtime, to look over the child's shoulder when she was doing her homework, to ruffle her hair, and only to yawn inconspicuously when she told them briefly about her day. They managed not to go to their bedroom, in spite of being tired, but instead to stretch out on the less comfortable sofa. They told the child they were just going to shut their eyes for a moment, and if anything should happen, and so the child finished her homework and went around the house on tiptoe and in stocking feet.

But the child is big now. I am big now.

FAMILY. AT HOME.

Louise Helene Waldmann.
Louisie. Lou. Lulu. Sweetie.

Seventeen years old. Old enough, at last, to get a driving licence. ('Rubbish, a driving licence? What do you want that for? You can go anywhere by bus in this town, or on your bike.')

Mother: nurse, in the local hospital. ('Yes, the hours, but it's all right, it's worked out OK.')

Father: electrician, caretaker, employed in the same hospital.

('Oh, well, electricity's my thing, really, but, you know, whatever, do you follow me? I mean, it might be that a water pipe bursts or something. I could be called in. But, you know, you get on with it, you learn as you go along. It's nothing to make a fuss about.')

No brothers or sisters. School certificate, fourth year, average mark B. I live in a small house with a small garden, with strawberries. A lawn, on which I played little games when I was little myself.

When my parents talk about the house and the garden and the nearness of their workplace, they forget to mention something: that the house is in the shadow of the hospital, opposite the graveyard. There's a little chapel there, which has a loud bell, and even on the twentieth floor of the hospital, the bell can be heard, when they bury someone.

And up there, they stand around in their bathrobes, on the balcony, they hang onto the rail, they stand there in their slippers and look down. And the higher up a person is, the less they have to do with it, the less anyone up there thinks that, down here, that could be me there in the coffin.

And in the meantime, my parents have a layer of hard skin over their ears. You can hear the bells here, hear the ambulance sirens, and they've gradually ceased to be shocked when the sirens go wailing past our house, when the bells toll for someone who's passing over into eternity.

My parents also have a layer of hard skin over their eyes. You notice it when they look at you. They say it's because they are so tired. It's those tired eyes that can only be prised open at work after two cups of coffee, one for each eye. I only see them at home. I don't see them at all. Sometimes they're here. Sometimes one of them is lying on the sofa or in bed. Sometimes one of them comes back from the shop, puts the bags on the kitchen table and calls me to unpack and put the stuff away and then they have to go off again. Once a week, someone cleans the bathroom, the kitchen, sometimes, occasionally, the windows. Someone does the lawn, if necessary. Everything gets done.

How quiet it is here!

SUMMER HOLIDAYS

So what are you doing for the summer? Are you going away? To the seaside? To friends? Are you going on a language course? Will you work in your father's business? And hang around at the waterhole the rest of the time? Or are you going to that festival?

Three people have asked me what I am doing this summer.

1: My grandmother

'Louisie, when are the holidays starting?'

'Next week.'

'So? Have you got anything planned?'

'Well, I need to earn some money and also I thought …'

'Listen, Louisie, I'm going to see Aunt Jette in Tuscany.'

'Mmmm?'

'Well, you know how it is. She has a problem with Bonnie.'

'Really? With Bonnie?'

'Oh, yeah. The latest is she claims she's allergic.'

'And she's not?'

'So I'm going on Monday. For four weeks, and I was just wondering if maybe you could take Bonnie for me? You get on so well with her. You're so good with dogs.'

'Em, well, I think I'd have to ask Mum …'

'Listen, I've already had a word with your mother. She says she just can't look after the dog but she doesn't mind if you do it. Look, you'll really be doing me a favour. I hardly ever get to go away.'

'I don't know …'

'Louisie, I'm not expecting you to do it for nothing. You're taking driving lessons, aren't you?'

'Yes?'

'If you take Bonnie, I'll make a contribution towards that. Well?'

'OK? Maybe …?'

'Fine! Come around on Sunday. I'll have everything packed. Around ten? OK? OK. I have to go and talk to my neighbour about the flowers. See you on Sunday, then. Bye, lovie.'

2. Nora from the B class

'So? Going away?'

'What?'

'On holidays?'

'Eh …'

'My bus! Shit, how come it's …?! So, have a good summer, OK?'

3. We used to sit together in the second-last period, which was a free class because they never found a substitute for the English teacher, who'd been sick for weeks. 'Nervous breakdown,' the teachers whispered behind their hands. 'Loony bin,' we said, and, 'She's flipped.' So we sat around the radiator in the corridor, because they didn't want to let us go home because we had maths last class and because the canteen was closed. And who goes to the library when you can't talk there? Back warm from the heating, sub-zero temperatures for weeks, and the floor, even through the jacket I was sitting on,

on which you sat with me, still noticeably cold, because, after all, it is stone. There we sat, in the winter, at the beginning of January, our shoulders and knees touching. One of my hands in your two big dry hands, you holding it as if I had something amazing there at the end of my arm. But it was only a hand. And you looked at each finger, my hand, your hands and the warm radiator. Warm shoulders and backs, and the question about the summer, about train tickets that you can go right across Europe on. 'I have a tent,' you said, and I thought it was time I had a new sleeping bag, that of course we could do it, just go off together, not for ten days at summer camp, but for weeks.

The summer is a long time off when it's only January and then February and March come and sometimes it snows even as late as April. It didn't snow in April. The weather forecasters pointed incredulously at the weather map. And it was spring, winter over. It's funny how everything melts away when the spring comes.

JOB 1: BAKED GOODS

'Go to the Corner Bakery,' my gran said when she heard I was looking for a job, because my gran knows the baker and because everyone who has children heads off for the summer and they need staff to cover.

So I go to the Corner Bakery, and he asks if I can do everything. If I can use a till. And if I've ever worked in a shop before. I fudge it a bit and say, 'Yes, but it was a while ago.' Because serving at the wedding of a friend's sister is in the first place not shop work and secondly it's not using a till and in the third place it isn't even a good while ago. But it was a job, I was tired after it and I got money for it and I stank of sweat.

The corner baker is called Reinhardt. 'Reinhardt's Bakery' it says outside, he sells bread, which is baked behind the shop, and coffee, in beans, but also freshly ground. The Corner Bakery is called that because there used to be another baker called Reinhardt, only he wasn't at the corner, he was next to the Protestant church. The other baker doesn't exist any more but the church is still there, and so is the corner and the Corner Bakery too. It's survived, and it's a really traditional business that hasn't been bought out by some chain. The Corner Bakery has always had the same display in the window: a smiling sun made of dough and a little plastic baker, grinning stupidly, with bushy eyebrows. And along with that, flowers according to season, Easter bunnies, Christmas decorations, pumpkins. Corner Baker Reinhardt has a red face and a thick neck. He sweats, because it's hot outside, it's hot in here, and inside in the bakery itself, it's definitely hotter still. We sit in the kitchen behind the shop, you can sit there for a moment when there's nothing doing. But only for a moment. If someone looks in the shop window and nobody is on duty, what kind of impression does that make?

'The shop opens at six in the morning, which means you have to be here at half past five, because the baked goods have to be set out. And then it's all go until lunch time. Five days a week,' he says, not looking at anyone. Waits. How can coffee go cold when it's so warm? How come water gets warm but coffee still goes cold? Or am I just imagining it? And because I don't answer and because I don't say, 'What? Five days a week? I don't want to work as much as that,' he says a changeover happens at midday, the takings are counted, a note is taken of what's been sold, the subtotal is printed out. Everything is checked, and only when it all balances am I allowed to go. He looks again. The coffee gets cold in summer too. He takes a slug, wipes his mouth, announces how much I am to be paid, waits a bit, and says: 'So, from six o'clock in the morning until one in the afternoon, that's seven hours, and three weeks until Mrs Savarin comes back, and then we'll see.'

He's just about to get up when I say, 'But I start at half past five.'

He raises his eyebrows and a frown creases his red forehead and he says, 'So what?'

'Well, that's seven and a half hours.'

He doesn't answer.

'So, not just seven hours. As far as I am concerned.'

He lays a hand flat on the table, leans towards me and says, 'That's how we do it here. The others have no problem with it. The evening shift has to stay back to clean up after everyone else has finished.'

The only thing that occurs to me is 'But'. I suppress it, he nods, straightens up, puts out his hand to me, says, 'So, if that's all clear?' and I nod.

'So you start on Monday. Mrs Marquard has the key, she'll open up.'

I take his hand and leave my coffee to get cold.

JOB 2: NEWS PRESS

Jonas is at the door.

'Hey,' I say.

'Hey.'

'What's up?'

'Do you need a job, by any chance?'

'Why?'

'I have one for you.'

'What kind of job?'

'Holiday cover. For me. Delivering newspapers.'

'For how long?'

'I'll be away for four weeks. It mounts up. But I can't just go away for four weeks. They don't let you do that, I'd lose my job.'

'But I'm working mornings already.'

'From what time?'

'From half five. At the Corner Bakery.'

'You'd be done by then, all free.'

'What do you mean, free? When would I have to do the delivery?'

'Well, the papers are at my door by four o'clock.'

'At four?'

'Yes, and the round takes about an hour. On foot.'

And then he mentions an amount for the month, and I am persuaded.

'I'll draw you a map of the route and I'll bring you the keys, OK?'

Four o'clock. Jonas raises his hand, goes, door closes. Four o'clock. It's doable.

THEORY

It's all down to planning. That's it, really, just a question of planning. If I set off in the morning shortly before four, I can take Bonnie for her first walk of the day. I've walked the route, I can manage it within an hour. Then I can take Bonnie home,

himself a coffee and going to the beach. I have the sheet with the names and the house numbers, everything copied three times so I won't forget anything because a sheet of paper can go missing. You have to think of every eventuality. Keys for the houses where there are letter-boxes in the lobby so I don't have to ring on any doors and annoy anyone. I've sorted the keys and marked them with different coloured plastic, so I don't have to be searching for hours for the right key. I have little plastic bags with me so that I can pick up the dogshit and throw it away, and Bonnie wees and Bonnie shits and I get rid of the shit, Bonnie waddles on, I deliver the newspapers, I keep an eye on the time, I'm well on schedule, I find all the houses, I've done my homework. Ha, homework! I give a short laugh into the night, because, like it's homework, work with homes … but if nobody laughs with you, it's not really all that funny. And then there's this house with a lot of letter-boxes, a paper for Schlegel, one for Müller, and there's only one Müller, but there are two Schlegels, A. Schlegel and then just Schlegel. I stand there and look from A. Schlegel to Schlegel, look at my list to see what it says. It says that Schlegel in Goethestrasse 5 gets a newspaper. Does that mean that Schlegel with no A. in front of it gets a paper, or is it the one with the A? Has Jonas just forgotten that there's more than one because he's been doing this job for a few years now, knows it all off by heart, only put the list together for me. After all, he knows which letter-box he has to throw the paper into, maybe it never even occurred to him that there are two Schlegels. Maybe one of them has only been here for a short while, and maybe he just said to himself, OK, well then, I'll just put the initial of my first name in front of my surname. Like A for Arthur, Anatol, Annegret, Angelika, aaaagh! Damn, and I can't be making mistakes, the newspaper company isn't supposed to know that I'm doing it. If they find out that Jonas has sort of sublet his job to me, then he'll lose it. But he needs it, otherwise he'd have taken the risk of telling them that he needs four weeks … goddammit, what am I going to do now?

I look at my watch, I still have a whole street to do. Well, then, just Schlegel, without A., it makes more sense, and then let's go, even if Bonnie is panting along the street, quick, no Bonnie, you can't sniff at that flower just because another dog has gone by and left a scent behind, dammit, come on! And so I drag Bonnie along the rest of the route, and at the end, I've worked my way through the list, and I see I have three papers left over. How come I've got three papers left? I did everything right, I did, didn't I? Haven't a clue, but because my conscience is pricking me, I go back to Goethestrasse 5, running, because now time is getting a bit tight. Open the door and then stick a paper also into A. Schlegel's letter-box, and then home, quick. Bonnie off the lead, into the kitchen, water in one bowl, crunchies in the other one, quick hand-wash, they're black, newsprint-black, strange doors, dog, quick, quick, let's go, oh yes, take the bike, even if the light is broken, but the sun is coming up and anyway, what about it, the police aren't going to be out, are they? No. When I arrive at the baker's, he's standing there in the shop looking at a list, counting things. I go running in, hardly stopping to throw my things into the cubbyhole behind, yank my shop-coat from the hook and wriggle into it. 'You're late,' says the boss. No time to answer.

Mrs … damn, how come I can't remember her name? says I have to get an order ready for the old people's home, gives me a list and shows me how I'm supposed to sort it all, but from where? Oh, right, from there. And look at her hands, because I think, just by hand, yes, with your bare hand, so, right. So I count out rolls and loaves and then more rolls. And the boss stands there beside me the whole time. He's practically tapping his foot, he's waiting so loudly, and the more I count and tick off the list, the louder he waits. But then it's all ready and he loads up the van that's outside the door and then he's gone. When the van is no longer to be seen, the woman turns to me, holds out her hand and says, 'I'm Angela.' A. Schlegel, I think, but she's not called Schlegel. 'Hello, Louise.'

'The coffee is brewed,' says Angela. 'Would you like a cup? Everything is all set up already. Come on, get yourself a cup of coffee.'

I do that. Outside it's getting bright and I realise how badly I need the coffee.

And then at some stage it becomes routine. On the second day, you still look at the list. On the third day only to double-check. On the fourth, you just remember.

AND ON THE FIFTH

It is so hot at lunchtime, so unbelievably hot, that I walk as slowly as Bonnie. Not only her stomach and ears are trailing on the ground but even her tongue, which is hanging out of her mouth.

We make our way around the house, then all along Müllerstraße, up the street. I'm trying to find every scrap of shade but the sun is so high in the sky that only trees cast shadows, and there aren't any trees, any big, spreading trees, on Müllerstraße. I think of the graveyard, it'll surely be cool there, but I can't go there with Bonnie, dogs aren't allowed there. Especially piddling and crapping dogs. Bonnie lifts her leg, sprinkles the wall with a few miserable drops, shuffles and waddles on. Snuffles again, snuffles here, there and everywhere, scavenging pointlessly. It's so hot. I've forgotten my sunglasses, screw up my eyes, my forehead is dripping with sweat, and my armpits, it's tired sweat. 'Come on, Bonnie, do a poop for goodness sake, I want to go home,' I say, but Bonnie is snuffling on, dragging me after her on the stupid lead all along

Müllerstraße. At some point, she stops in the middle of the footpath, goes down slowly on wobbly knees, and I look in my bag for the crap-bags. Forgot them. That's just great. Used the last one this morning and forgot to stick in some new ones. And the pile of shit is pretty well in the middle of the path. Not even on the edge, where you might have some chance of not stepping right into it. Bonnie drags me along again, and I think, What the hell, other people do it.

'Hey!' someone shouts.

I turn around, but I can't see anyone.

'Hey! You can't just leave that crap in the middle of the pavement like that!'

But there's no-one there. Oh God, it's happened, I've got sunstroke, I'm hearing things, the dead people are calling me from the graveyard.

'HEY! I'm talking to you!'

And then I see a girl sitting up on one of those electricity boxes, however the hell she got up there. I hold my hand up to shade my eyes so that I can get a better view of her.

'So, are you going to get rid of it or aren't you?'

'Nah.'

'And what if someone steps in it?'

'What difference is it to you?'

'Well, suppose I step in it?'

'You? You know it's there.'

'That doesn't make things better, does it?'

The girl is maybe thirteen. But tall and thin, almost skinny, with short black hair, and she's sitting up there with her legs crossed. Eating cake.

'What are you doing anyway?'

'I'm the pavement police. You are going to be formally cautioned.' She points at the shit. 'That is to be removed at once, or you'll get a caution, and not only because of the shit, but for negligence of a person in charge.'

'Ignoring.'

'What do you mean, ignoring?'

'Negligence doesn't make any sense.'

'No way. If I step into it, slip and break something, then that's dangerous negligence. Homicide.'

Then she sticks her piece of cake in her mouth, smears the chocolate around her mouth, chews, it's a chocolate cake and I feel sick. 'Come on, Bonnie, let's go.'

'Hey!'

I go on, I really want to get home, yesterday I didn't pass one single sample test sheet, there are always a couple of mistakes too many, I want to drink something, go into my room, it's cool there, the shutters are down, then I'll sleep for a bit and do a few more test sheets before my driving lesson so that I can finally …

'Hey, you can't just push off like that!'

The girl is really tall. I'm seventeen, and she can look me effortlessly in the eye. She's standing in front of me, she has grey eyes with a black ring around the iris. 'That's hit and run. D'you know what that means?'

'You should put on a hat. The sun isn't doing you any good.'

'Huh? Cheeky too? Listen, missy, I'm warning you – if I have to report this …!'

She's loopy. I want to go home, but Bonnie seems to be ten kilos heavier. I snarl at her, she looks back gormlessly at me, and the girl bends over and strokes her fat head. 'You're cute. Is she yours?' Bonnie suddenly snaps awake and offers the paw.

'Listen, kid, I have no time, I have to get home. Enjoy your little game of police. And goodbye.' I turn around and march the few metres to our house, drag Bonnie in and close the door.

Jana

THIRTEEN

It can't be. She can't have forgotten what day it is today. When I woke up, Mum had already left, working, like always, but then, then I went into the kitchen and there just like always a note on the kitchen table: 'See you at the hospital.' On the table a plate, a cup and a pot of tea. That disgusting oolong tea. Yucky tea. She knows I don't like it. There's nothing on the table but breakfast, and all the note says is that we'll see each other at the hospital.

No candle? No candle. No cake, no biscuits. No card. She can't have forgotten. I look outside. It's summer out there, a lovely hot day. It's my birthday.

I spent the day in the garden, opened the patio door, pushed the speakers up against the door and listened to loud music. I put on my big sunglasses and my little bikini, lay on a blanket and drank lemonade. I left the tea in the kitchen. I pretended that I was house-sitting, that I'm older, that I'm doing it to earn a bit extra during the holidays. That it's someone else's house. With neighbours who peer over the hedge and think I'm sexy, but whom I ignore. I looked at all the magazines I've bought over the last few months, but I didn't learn anything from them. I wanted to go on daydreaming, but then the post came, so I ran indoors, nearly slipped, but only nearly, to check the post. But it was boring, loads of stupid rubbish and a card from Granny Thesi, which said something religious and cutesy on it, and then all this stuff about how hard it is these days and she hopes that all the same and chin up and so on. And everything else was all about Tom, so I threw the card in the bin.

It was still bright and warm in the garden, but somehow I wasn't able to go on daydreaming any more. The lemonade had got warm too and something was swimming in it. And then old Meinert started mowing the lawn, long and loud. So I went inside and changed the TV channel, but there was nothing on, so I went online but nobody had sent me a message. They're all away, I suppose, all on holidays, all except us. I did ask what we were doing about holidays, but no, how could we, and how could I even think about such a thing with Tom and everything. Not even some youth camp, so I showered the garden off myself and made myself pretty. I'm thirteen after all, a teenager, not a child any more, and everyone else was allowed to put on makeup at thirteen. Aise in the B class has been using makeup since we were in sixth. And she's Turkish.

So I smartened myself up, washed my hair, put some cream on, noticed how white those bits are that were covered by the bikini, and how brown the rest of me is all around. Felt kind of proud that I can tan right here, without having to go to Costa

Somewhere, nah, pure central-German garden tan. So then I got all my makeup stuff out of my room and set it all up in the bathroom, there's more space there, didn't have to push things aside or put them away. Did my eyes, my mouth, put a bit of shimmer here and there, it looked good, my hair is just short, can't do much with that, but my face was good.

So then I left at some stage, because Mum finishes at three, and then she's there really quickly, because she's waiting for me, and especially now I don't have to go to school. So, when I get there, I see Dad's car in front of the hospital, think, good, so at least they're both here. So maybe they have remembered that I've turned thirteen, and they can wish me a happy birthday, the two of them together, pull themselves together. I was even looking forward to it, no need to hang around at the reception desk in the waiting area. Then I go upstairs, open the door, Dad looks up, Mum looks up, Tom's wrist in her hands, like every day, telling him something about work, telling him about the neighbours, looks up and says, 'What have you done?'

And I don't know what she's talking about.

Dad gives me a disappointed look.

'What?' I ask.

'You look like you're going to a carnival.' And shakes her head. Dad gives a little laugh, till Mum gives him a look and nods towards Tom, who's lying there and who can't possibly care what I look like.

'Wash yourself,' says Mum looking towards the bathroom.

And nobody mentions that it's my birthday, that I'm thirteen now, that it's good to see me, and mainly because Tom is just lying around. He's been lying there for weeks, more weeks than a month, nearly two in fact. But here I am and I'm a year older and I'm not a child any more, and so I can look like this, and I can look at them and talk to them, but Mum is still looking towards the wash basin there in the little bathroom which Tom doesn't use anyway, and they don't wish me a happy birthday, because at last I am thirteen and large as life. And nothing has changed. Not even after I'd washed my face and my skin taut from the soap. Nothing, not even from Dad. He patted me briefly on the head, but so briefly that you'd hardly even notice it. And then we sit there, and time crawls by like on every afternoon around Tom's bed, because Mum and Dad always talk the same old shite about work, about some friends who send their best but can't be here. At some stage I'm going to have to tell what I've been doing. 'Apart from getting yourself up like that,' says Mum, and Daddy says, 'Marion!' which Mum ignores.

'Dunno,' I say.

'Jana's on holidays now,' Mum says to Tom.

Tom's on holidays now too, I want to say, and it's Jana's birthday, but there's no cake.

'So, petal, what did you do today then?' asks Dad.

'I was in the garden.'

'Tom, the garden, it's so lovely just now, everything is in flower. I have to put on the sprinkler every evening, because it's so hot, but I haven't lost anything,' says Mum.

I think, He doesn't give a shit about the garden.

'Come on, Jana, tell Tom something.'

I'd like to tell YOU something, Dad, I am thinking. But I only ever see him here, because either he's at work, or he's sitting around here and then he goes home in the evening.

And not to our house.

I shrug. 'Why? It's just a day like any other. Isn't it?' Then I stare at them both thinking, It's my birthday today, today is my bloody birthday.

But all Mum says is, 'Jana, if you're in such a bad mood, you may as well leave. I can't be doing with that here.'

Dad says nothing, because Mum would ignore him anyway.

She looks at the door and then at me until I leave.

Actually it's quite good that I've washed, because it would only get smeared anyway. A nurse passes me, whose name I should know, because she knows mine and because Mum says it's rude that I forget the names of most grown-ups. The nurse puts on a sympathetic face, but she hasn't a clue, she's only thinking about Tom, says: 'Who knows, maybe he'll wake up soon.' And has no idea that I'd like to shake her.

I'm hungry. I go to the vending machines on the second

floor because the one on Tom's floor only has stupid stuff. The one on the second floor has these round chocolate cakes, which have this white fondant in the middle. So I get myself one, go outside, because it stinks here and because I'm cold here. Up here on the electricity box nobody can see me. I rip the cake out and look at it and I feel sad-angry-cross-everything because I haven't got a candle so I can't make a wish. I don't even want to cry. Everyone just cries. Always, all the time. Either they cry or they fight or they separate or they keep quiet, say nothing and think a lot and don't want to be disturbed.

I don't want sad any more.

I bite into the cake and decide I am going to enjoy it. And then along comes this dog.

I like dogs.

Louise

MIDDAY DISTURBANCE

The doorbell rings, someone is knocking. I've just closed my eyes, I'm lying down in my room, the shutters have been lowered in such a way that the light from the garden throws ovals on the wall. Think, it's nobody important. And if it is important, then whoever it is will come back. Bonnie looks up lazily from her blanket. Bonnie hasn't barked when someone comes to the door for the last couple of years. She rests her head on her paws again.

Ringing. Knocking.

Pretty soon he or she will give up and go. I don't have to get up.

Ringing and knocking. And then I suddenly hear a voice through the front door, through the hall, through the door of my room. Whoever is outside the door has a pretty loud voice.

Maybe something has happened. So I jump up, pull on my trousers, a shirt, go to the door, yank it open. It's the kid from earlier, saying, 'Hey! Oh, it's lovely and cool in here!' She raises a hand and tries to slip past me. But I am not going to stand for that. 'Listen, are you mad?'

She sticks out her hand to me and says, 'Hi, I'm Jana. And

you're Louise. And you can let me in now, I'm not a stranger any more.'

'How come you know my name?'

'We go to the same school. You're in fourth year, right? I'm in first year. In 1C.'

'So?'

'Do you like cake?'

'Not as much as you do, apparently.'

Jana looks questioningly at me.

'Your face is all chocolate.'

'Oh! So where's the bathroom? Here? Ha, I knew it! Guest loos are always beside the front door.'

She goes ahead, me following.

She turns on the tap and asks, 'So, will you come?'

'Where?'

'Tea-party. I'm inviting you! Oh, and can we bring the dog?'

'Actually, I have something on.'

'It's my birthday.'

'Happy birthday.'

Jana dries her mouth with the little towel and looks in the mirror, passes her tongue over her teeth. 'Fine. I'm clean again. So then we can go.'

She catches me suddenly by the hand, runs into the hall, and Bonnie trots along. 'Who's a good dog?'

I shake off her hand. 'I have no time! How often do I have

to tell you! So it's your birthday, that's great, but you'll have to ask someone else to your tea-party, because I have no time.'

'Oh. OK. Pity.'

Jana looks out the door, then she looks at me again and paints a smile across her mouth. 'Well, then. Till tomorrow. Bye.'

And goes.

I stand in the hall and Bonnie wags and wags her tail. Then I close the door. Till tomorrow? I go back into my room, the bed is cool. I pull the sheet over me, wait. Hear Bonnie settling down, turning over, giving a sigh, then peace descends.

I lie there for a good while, waiting for sleep, but it won't come. At some stage I look at the clock by the bed and get up to do a few more test papers.

Jana

COMING HOME

I've been gadding about, I want to tell her, when I get home. Mum, I've been gadding about, I was here for a long time, and then I was there for a good while and after that I was in that other place. Did you know, Grover in Sesame Street, he always wanted to be there, but that was never going to happen, but it was fun.

I walked around the city centre, I bought myself a dress, nicked something. Nobody noticed, here, this ring, the little silver one, at one of those stalls, nobody saw, really, it was almost sad, actually, that nobody noticed. Mum, I hung out, I was outside, nowhere to go, nothing planned. I didn't ring you to ask if I should pick-up/bring-home something from the market, from Aldi, from the shoemaker or whatever while I was out and about.

I was just out, and the ring is far too small, it only fits my pinky, it's way too small, but I nicked it, and nobody noticed. I sat down by the river for a while. I ate an ice-cream and there were these people playing music, smoking weed, and I waved at them but they were probably too drunk or something. I'd love to have sat with them and shared my ice-cream with them, shown them the ring, and maybe they'd even have sung Happy Birthday to me, it can't be that hard for someone who plays the guitar.

And then I walked around, further and further, blowing kisses to the builders with the beer bellies on Rheinstraße, they laughed and whistled waved at me too. I wandered around. I didn't go home. And I'll tell you something else, if you ask. I'll tell you something or other and the ring, you won't even notice it.

THE TOM THING

'We'll take the car,' says Mum, even though it's only to go to the supermarket. Two minutes on foot, but no, we'll take the car. And sometimes we go out of our way, we don't go shopping around the corner but to the big supermarket, the one off the motorway. We load up the car, full to bursting, and then we can take a break for a week, maybe two. Mum says there's no point in running around from one shop to another for every little crappy thing. And that you have it all here. And if there are any bits and bobs, I can go for them. Off you go, Jana, go like a good girl and get. And says it's because I hardly ever go out, it's good for me to bestir myself. And because she can't be bothered with every crappy little thing, she does work, and then there's the hospital and all that. I can easily go around the corner to the supermarket, I'm old enough after all. And I can explain to the people all about the Tom thing, because it just wears her out, all the ins and outs and the girl at the till, and everyone knows that we're the family with Tom, they've all read it in the paper. So they say to me: 'Jana, pet, tell me, how's your brother doing these days, any change? And your mother?' And as soon as I turn my back, pointed looks, headshaking, whispering, muttering behind their hands. Because of course how could I know, and the mother won't give anything away. Then as I move on a couple of steps, how could it have happened? It's not as if he went around in black all the time, like the Schneiders' Jannek. In his case, well, with him you could well imagine it. But Tom? 'Who was that again?' someone asked. You know, the boy, so-and-so tall and his hair such and such a colour and he always had things on and he'd help people with things. Because everyone has something to say about Tom. Him? Surely not him! Headshaking, incredulous. But it's always the quiet ones. And Tom, so healthy, rosy cheeks. Played sport and all.

'Was he not?'

Yes, he was a long distance runner. WAS. USED TO BE. Therefore healthy. Everyone knows, mens sana and so on. So what was the problem? The parents? Divorced? Drink? Antisocial? No, they both work, seem to have money. Separated, yes, but maybe there was something in the past, children can sense that kind of thing.

And computer games, did he? Or that loud music with the awful lyrics? It's well known! But they don't usually hurl themselves off a bridge, they run riot.

One says: 'Well, better that.' Better that he throws himself off the bridge than that he gets others mixed up in his misery. No. And was there a suicide note? Shrugs. Nobody knows anything about a letter. Terrible, a thing like that. The poor mother. You never see her any more. Off what bridge? What? That one? And he survived that?

Yes. He did. Survived it. Anyone else would have been in bits. Anyone else would be six feet under by now. But Tom was too good for that. Too fit.

Tom, with his above-average body, somehow defied gravity. No, Tom doesn't die. Tom survives and there he lies.

'That's no joke either,' says one woman, and that everyone knows it's not going to be getting any better. Someone knows a family who sank a lot of money into a thing like that, hospital and then rehab and so on, no, they went bankrupt. Well, they did. Don't you know?

But why? Always it comes back to why.

'Did he not say anything to you?' my granny asked. No, nothing. And didn't leave a letter, they've gone through all his emails and Facebook and Twitter. Nothing. No girlfriend who broke up with him, no bullying, no comment, no status that could have given anything away. No nothing. No one could have had the foggiest idea.

And now he's lying there and nobody can ask him any more.

And if Mum says, Jana, go and get two litres of milk, I just plug my music in my ears, and it's fine.

ESCAPADE

I was at the lake.

Got up in the morning and it was so warm, so unbelievably warm, I wanted water, and not with chlorine. So I got out the map and looked up how to get there. Packed myself some biscuits and a fizzy drink, put on bathing things, sunglasses, hat, flip-flops. Change of underwear, straw mat, towel, music, sun-cream. My bus pass, stuffed in some money behind it and then off. Took a bus, then another, then waited. Then another bus came, took me a bit further, got out, walked the rest of the way, sandy path, a few trees, shade. Followed the signs to the lake, and suddenly it was there, and just the way it should be. Was even a beach for me and my things, wasn't all alone, a family near by, I asked them if they'd keep an eye on my things, while I'm in the water. Sure. And I was swimming, dived, sliced through the water, forwards, backwards, without even getting water up my nose. And then out and dry again. And eyes closed and listening and a little nap. Then too warm, so back into the water, and like that the whole time, getting wet, drying off, being dry, into the water again.

At some stage the family goes, but others take their place.

Then someone comes by with an ice-cream in his hand and says, 'Jana?'

And I put up a hand to shade my eyes, I haven't a clue who it is. But I say 'Hi' anyway.

And he hunkers down, and then it's easier to see him, but I still don't know him. Then he says, 'You're Tom's little sister, aren't you?'

'Yes,' I say, but I don't see in his face what I see in everyone else's, the ones who follow up by saying, 'What a sad story that is' and how is he and how are my parents and bad-bad-bad-bad.'

'I'm Fabian, remember? Tom and I were friends in fifth class.'

And not after that?

'Then we moved away,' he says and sits down. 'So how's Tom? What's he doing these days?'

He has no idea, I realised, and how could he, it wouldn't have done the rounds out here. What would people out in the country care about something that happened in the city several weeks ago?

'School.'

'Ah. So he went on to secondary? Is he doing his final exam?' I nod.

He pulls up a bit of grass and rubs it between his fingers.

I ask: 'And you?'

'I've started an apprenticeship.'

'Yes?'

'Insurance salesman. I know, sounds boring, but it's not too bad. I want to do my school exam too at some stage. But first I need to earn some money.'

I nod. I'm warm again.

'Are you here on your own?'

Nod again.

'Look, I'm sitting over there with a few friends, come on over.'

Fabian is a good name, I think, and it's OK to go with a Fabian. So I take my things.

'How old are you now? Fourteen? Fifteen?'

'Nearly sixteen,' I say.

'Cool. And Tom didn't want to come with you to the lake?'

'Nah, he's not at home right now.'

'Ah, so where is he?'

'He's travelling. I mean, he has a job in Japan.'

'Japan, really? Wow.'

'Yeah, he got it through friends of my father's. And afterwards, he wants to travel around for a bit.'

'Gosh, Japan!' says Fabian coming to a halt. Points around and says a few names, there's a couple of boys, three girls, who are looking at something, can't see where, they're wearing big sunglasses. Someone asks if I'd like a beer. I say: 'Later maybe.'

And put my things down somewhere, don't want to sit, though. Fabian looks at me, he's finished his ice-cream ages ago, and says that he's going into the water now, who's coming? The girls don't budge, the boys are opening beers and are sweating. So I go with him. Swimming and diving and at this stage Tom has learnt Japanese and has written to say that he's met a girl there, might even study there. And I'm glad that Fabian doesn't ask exactly where in Japan Tom is, because I know nothing about Japan. Asks what I'm doing and what school I'm at. I say something about a boarding school, in case he knows someone who would be in my class if I am nearly sixteen. So I'm at a boarding school somewhere in Bavaria. He does ask where but I say: 'You wouldn't know it.'

'Gee, and what's that like?'

'OK,' I say, acting cool as a cucumber and tell about how liberal it is and how we call the teachers by their first names and how we go to class in our pyjamas sometimes and so on. And about parties.

And when we go back to the beach, I lie down and I have my sunglasses on too and I let on to be tired and sleeping and just listen. But the boys aren't too interested and the girls even less so. Somehow it's evening, and I've forgotten to check how late the buses run.

'We're going back to my place to have a barbecue,' says Fabian.

And wouldn't I like to come, there's room in his car, and I say yes, no problem, my parents aren't expecting me anyway. He looks at me curiously, until I say that I had been planning to visit friends but that I can go on there later because a barbecue sounds super.

The girls weren't talking to me, but that was OK, the boys were going on drinking and talking about the barbecue and which is the right way to put the meat on the grill. And gradually it got dark. I did think that I really should be home by now. I wondered briefly what I'd do if Mum asked me how come I wasn't there when she got home, how on earth I was even going to get home and where exactly I was. And then Fabian made me a shandy. I don't actually like beer much, but mixed with Sprite it's delicious and refreshing and there was sausage too. After a day like that at the lake, you can be pretty peckish. And then some more people came. And then Fabian's mother was there, she came and sat at some stage with the girls and she'd hugged one of them. Had Fabian got a sister? I wondered. And it was dark and music and tomato salad, good and sharp, that, and someone played the guitar, that was lovely. And only Fabian knew Tom and he'd stopped asking questions, so that was good. And a shandy tastes very good too, a big, cold shandy. And another one, after the sausage and with the salad.

And then I went wandering around. Through the big

garden, there was a pond and a garden swing.

I sat into it and looked up and swung. Everything so still and quiet, in me and in the sky.

And then Fabian came, put another beer in my hand, one without Sprite, but it didn't taste too bad at all. And we sat there and said nothing, and at one point he took my hand. Possibly nothing at all happened, just a bit of hand-holding, and maybe he moved in a bit closer.

But maybe it was a bit too much beer all the same. And Fabian hasn't got a sister at all, but a girlfriend, who suddenly appeared and started crying and then ran away. I had no idea what she wanted. Then Fabian went after her, but she came back and shouted at me. And other girls were there and his mother too, said I should go.

'I have to get into town somehow,' I said and that I live near the West Station. She snorted and said that was the limit, what I had just suggested.

But Fabian said, 'Please, Mum.' Because the others weren't going into town and the bus had gone ages ago, the last one.

The woman took her keys and went to a car, I found my things somewhere.

After one, two kilometres, she started complaining, about me, and how I'm such a hussy and about men and how could women do such a thing? I couldn't really follow her, I was dizzy, because it all happened too fast, and I don't much like driving at night. Then she started smoking and I tried to open the window, because I'd gone from dizzy to sick. But that didn't help.

So then I asked her to stop and I got out and took two steps, then another couple, breathed and looked around. Then she threw my things out of the car and drove off, in the middle of the night and I don't even know where I am. She didn't come back either. I waited there, but she didn't come back.

The good thing about the summer is that the night doesn't last long. At some stage it just gets light, even if you haven't had a wink of sleep, if you are somewhere else and don't know where. The first thing is to walk along the road.

And if you walk along a road long enough, then at some stage there's a village, if you're lucky there's a shop open where they'll sell you a hot chocolate and say, yes, there's a bus stop here, but there's no bus at the weekend. But if you just keep going along the main road out of town and a bit further, after three kilometres you come to the next village, and there by the church, there's a bus that goes even on Saturdays.

Louise

COUNTRY DRIVE

'On Saturday we'll do the country drive,' says Kehrer. Him? Yes, him, his wife is going on a different trip. 'Is that a problem?' he says.

'Sure, no problem.'

So I'm picked up at eight, well awake by then. Newspapers and dog, and now it's not so hot. Remembered my sunglasses, cough sweets and tissues, I'm all set. So then at eight he drives up, gets out, the car is doing an empty trip, so it's empty, shake hands, in I get, seat forward, seat back a bit, finally the seat is right, mirrors, rear-view mirror, wing mirrors, yes, everything's fine, engine running, he gives me a nod, another look over my shoulder, indicator, and away. Thirty-kilometre zone. He says nothing, everything has gone OK, just lets me drive, then says that I should go right at the next crossroads. I do that, still says nothing, so I drive, then at some stage he says: 'And here please go straight ahead. We'll stick to the main road.' I know that he just wants to get out of the city. I know the drill.

At one point he gets a call, I try not to take any notice. His wife always has the radio on, not here. So on we go. And drive. He bends forward, roots in a plastic bag, takes out a sandwich. Salami. Wonder how many salami sandwiches the man eats in a week. He's had one on four trips out of six with me alone. That mounts up. But that can't be good. The whole car smells of salami. Then we're passing the last houses that are still part of the city. The last bus stop. From that point on I can get up a bit of speed, but need to watch out in case there's an 80 sign hidden somewhere. We've had all this before. Kehrer's snouting around. Stops addressing me politely, then suddenly calls me 'Girl!' as in: 'Whatcha doin', girl!' After that I'm Ms Waldmann again. That's OK. Was taken aback only the first time. I've heard it before and I know some people who've gone to a different driving school because of it, but then Kehrer is cheap. The next yellow sign we see says this suburb is part of the city, but it's not city-city any more. It's the sticks. Wouldn't want to live here.

So, pick up speed. Tractor on the road, going slowly. Going very slowly. Foot off brake, but can't overtake because there's a bend. And then there's a hill. Takes time. Till the tractor is over it. Takes time.

I start sweating because I don't know if I'll manage to do the overtaking thing before the next bend, which hasn't come into view yet, and so on. And I try and I make no headway. Kehrer is sure to start grumbling. Why the hell isn't the bloody car moving?

'So, Ms Waldmann, what was the problem?'

Nothing occurs to me off the top of my head.

'Have we got the radio on?'

What's he on about with the radio?

'No?'

'So what can we hear?'

And when I don't answer, the next question comes.

'So what gear are we in?'

Can I look down? Is it even possible to tell by looking?

'Fourth,' he answers. 'And what will we do now?'

'Come down a gear?'

'That might be an idea,' he says.

He's put two lessons back to back. So we drive on till we get to the arsehole of nowhere and then back again. Exactly the way we came.

This time no tractor, no complications. And the sun is shining, he has the window down. It would be nicer if we had music, but I'm not going to ask for that. At some point he mutters something into his beard that I don't understand, wonder for a moment if it was directed at me, but then he says: 'Weary of life!' and pretty loud too.

He looks around, says: 'Go a bit slower, girl,' so I slow down though I don't understand why.

'Please stop on the hard shoulder,' he says, because there's a girl walking along in front of us, and when we get closer, I can see what girl.

Then he gets out, goes towards her. She turns round, just

about to put out her thumb.

I can't hear what he's saying, all I know is he's loud and he's furious.

Kehrer has a little daughter. Around eight or nine. Probably he's gone into father mode, or maybe just road-safety mode. He's shouting. At one point, Jana looks past him and catches sight of me and waves. Kehrer turns around, sees me raising my hand. Then back to Jana.

The two of them come back to the car. Get in. Jana, behind, murmurs, 'Hello,' and then she looks out of the window.

'Ms Waldmann, do you know this young lady?'

I nod.

'Then maybe we'd best drive her home.'

For the next kilometre he mutters and mumbles into his beard, looks behind, but Jana goes on looking out of the window.

Finally he turns around, the whole bulky man, and snaps at her: 'Are you weary of life, girl?'

At that, Jana finally turns away from the window, I can just see this out of the corner of my eye, turns her head towards Kehrer and says very quietly: 'No. I'm not.'

'And how old are you?' asks Kehrer.

'Fifteen,' says Jana.

'Do your parents know where you're wandering around? At fifteen?'

'Yeah,' says Jana.

'And they let you go hitch-hiking? Don't make me laugh.'

'I was out on my bike. At the lake. And then they stole my mobile. And the bike. So I thought it wasn't such a long way, I was just making for the next bus stop. But it was further than I thought.'

Bullshit, I think.

'What lake were you at?' I ask.

'The resevoir.'

'Which one?'

'The one with the sand dunes around it.'

'And an island in the middle?'

'Yes, that's the one.'

Ha! The little liar.

'Mr Kehrer, there's a bus stop, I could stop there.'

'Ms Waldmann, we can take your friend all the way back, now that we have her here in the car.'

'Is that allowed, though? From an insurance point of view?' I ask.

Kehrer waves that off.

'Stolen?' he asks then over his shoulder.

'Yes and it was brand new. Got it as a birthday present. Had a really good lock too.

'I bet it was those Poles,' he says, rubbing his beard.

Jana

CURFEW

In films if someone sneaks out of the house, because he wants to go to a party, then he has to have a plan. Because in films, there's always a curfew. Or you're grounded. So they climb out of windows, and before that they put a doll or a big teddy with a wig on it under the blanket so their parents think that they're all tucked up in bed.

The fat driving instructor takes me home, or rather, Louise does. And doesn't even say goodbye.

So I arrive not having spent the night in my own bed.

Has Mum rung the police?

Is she sitting by the phone with red eyes waiting for a sign of life?

I take a deep breath, open the door and stand in the doorway.

And listen to the house.

Say: 'Hello.'

Say it again, louder: 'HELLO.'

Nothing.

'Mum?'

Then I close the door and go inside. It's all empty and quiet.

And my breakfast is in the kitchen and there's a note saying I'm to water the plants and to hoover. And the dishwasher: 'And empty the dishwasher, you were supposed to do that yesterday' (underlined three times).

I've been away for a day, and she hasn't even noticed.

So I take a shower and then I'm wet and then dry and clean and eat my breakfast and empty the dishwasher, put the dirty dishes in, and think to myself, she didn't even notice.

But I'm not grounded, and there's never been a mention of a curfew either, because I never really wanted to be out late. If there was a thing, a birthday or something, they always drove me there and picked me up again. And now I am thirteen and they haven't even noticed.

Does Mum not even look into my room when she gets home or before she goes to bed?

I look for my mobile. Mum has rung and left a voice message, but just to say that I should empty the dishwasher, and that she has to be at the office all day today. Even though it is Saturday.

Then I hoover, give the flowers a drink, wonder what to do next, look at the shopping list, but there's only milk on it. And for milk I don't need to go out.

I go into the garden, and the flowers are still alive. I pick a few raspberries from the cane and take a look at the currants, but they always look nicer than they taste.

And wonder what's possible if nobody checks whether I'm in bed. And suddenly the day is twenty-four hours long.

And then I want to know.

In the evening I'm in my room when Mum comes home, and she calls me, but I don't say anything. In my room it's dark and I'm sitting in a corner, my bed is made, not got up to look as if I'm in it. I'm waiting. It's nine o'clock in the evening. And Mum walks around the house and makes a phone call and looks at TV and then at some stage the TV goes off. Mum goes to the bathroom, knocks briefly on my door, softly, and says my name quietly, but I don't answer. The door doesn't open, the room stays dark, it is ten o'clock at night, and Mum goes to bed, thinking I am already asleep. And didn't listen to hear if I'm in the bathroom, didn't look to see if I'm in bed. Maybe took a look in the dishwasher or checked if the flowers have been watered, and sees that the vacuum cleaner has been put back into its cubbyhole differently from the way it was this morning.

And in the morning she gets up at five and at half past she has already left the house, although it's Sunday. And that's how it is every day. Sometimes she wants me to visit Tom, and says we'll see each other at the hospital But then I say I've been there already in the morning. And that I want to see Tom on my own. And sometimes I really do do that. And I sit for a while by his bed reading something. And say hello to the nurses, who say hello back and know my name. The nurses tell my parents that I've been there, and then they believe it's true when I say I see Tom in the mornings, even though I only do it once a week. And it doesn't occur to Mum that we haven't seen each other for a week. She writes me a note in the morning and I do what it says. And sometimes I really am there, when she's there, in the evening. But then I sit in my room and wait, wait and listen to her walking around the house, looking over the list of the day, ticking things off and deciding what I should do tomorrow and I wait and hear her watching TV, how she doesn't talk to Dad any more, hear her telephoning Granny sometimes and saying to her perhaps that I'm already in bed. And then she writes on the list, 'Ring Granny, she was asking for you yesterday.'

And wait, and Mum goes to bed and sometimes knocks and says my name softly. But she never comes in, not even once. And I sat there for a week, waiting for her to come in and see if I am still there. Sit by my bed, put a hand on my head to make sure that I am still there.

NIGHT SHIFT

And my room is on the ground floor. Can open the window. Can climb out without having to climb down on anything, without having to jump far. Just window open, out, past the lilac bush, don't even need to keep very quiet, because Mum won't hear me, she's asleep already. Don't close my jacket, it's not cold. Look at my watch, nearly midnight, twinkle, twinkle, little star. Nothing doing on my street, all very still and sleepy.

So I walk a bit, think, maybe I should take the bike after all, but it's in the garage, which I don't want to open. I walk. Maybe I'll take the bus. Or maybe not. Maybe there aren't any at this hour.

Walk to the main road, towards the city centre, which is not far, and walk. There are pubs, people still in them, though it's the middle of the week, but it's summer, that's probably why people stay up late.

What do people do at night? If you haven't got anything planned, then what do you do? I don't know how this kind of thing goes. What do people do if they stay up late at night, while other people are asleep, and not because they're watching a film or are going to a party?

I could go dancing. Maybe there's some place that is open where I could go, I like dancing. But would I get in? And where, anyway ? I could go into a pub. But I'm thirteen and I don't look eighteen. And don't know what I should do there. In a pub. You only get old fellows in places like that, sitting in front of their beers, looking around.

It's summer. And warm. Lots of people have their windows

open, and if they are watching TV then it's all blue. And sometimes I can hear music.

Then I'm in the old part of town, smells of pizza, and there are some people on the streets, going home, or going somewhere else, are not alone, walking together and have things to say to each other. And then there's music and someone is gathering chairs together. Outside it's being closed up, because people live around here, the streets are narrow and there's an echo and because the people who live here possibly don't want to hear music and talk. So they close up outside. And I walk behind some people, they're walking on, two of them are holding hands and they don't notice that I'm walking behind them. Then they go into a pub and then I walk behind the next person. They're going to the river, and there I can see there are more people and there's music. It's nice here. I shouldn't be anywhere near the river at night, I shouldn't be anywhere at night, should be at home asleep in my bed. But now I'm here and it's not spooky or dangerous. They're students, and they're sitting here and chatting and drinking and smoking. And have music with them. Twinkle, twinkle, little star, how I wonder what you are. And because it's dark, I'm brave enough to sit down beside them.

Decide I'm going to have my first smoke today, and I ask someone if he has a cigarette. He looks at me and says: 'Who's this on the scrounge? Cheeky!'

I say: 'Hi, I'm Stella.'

'Here, Stella, here's a cigarette for you.'

'And a light, can I have a light as well?' I ask.

'You can smoke it yourself, though, right?'

I say quickly: 'Sure, why?'

He laughs a bit, holds out a lighter to me, gives me a light, I give a careful pull and puff the smoke out immediately.

'Thanks,' I say and get up, because I know that the right way to smoke is to draw it into your lungs, and I'm going to have to try that out somewhere else. Say goodbye quickly and walk a bit until I can't see the group any more and then I sit on a bench.

This is how you smoke properly, pull, breathe in, 'Whouf, here comes Mum!' and I do that and have to cough, really badly need to cough. Why do they do it? Try again, less smoke, quickly whouf-here-comes-Mum cough-cough-cough.

It's no fun.

Then I get dizzy. No, not dizzy, light-headed. Not like drinking alcohol. Different, somehow. Is that what it's about?

So I'm smoking my first cigarette and trying to hold it properly and not look like it's my first cigarette.

And my head is light-light-light and then I walk a bit and the air is warm, fine, up above the world so high, like a diamond in the sky.

Hang around near another group for a while, listen,

and then walk further and at some stage I ask someone for a cigarette again and think, maybe it wouldn't be such a bad idea to have at least a light myself.

You can do that kind of thing in the summer, at night, when you should really be asleep.

You can smoke and be at the river. For example.

Of course I get tired. And go home, it's quite late into the night now, and I go home to my quiet street. I was at the river and nothing happened to me, I smoked and nothing happened to me.

Walk home, where my window is still open, so that I can climb back in, and lie down in bed and in my mouth still the taste of cigarettes.

Louise

NIGHTSHADE

It's the theory test today, but what does the newspaper care? The newspaper doesn't give a damn. The newspaper will be printed and delivered no matter what, the bundle of newspapers is in front of the door again, where it is every morning, the newspaper has to be delivered, whether or not I have a theory test. Even if my boss, for that's what the Corner Baker is called these days, my boss, even if he has given me a few hours off this morning. Generously. 'Well, I wouldn't be like that,' he said, because the bloody theory test is on in the morning, because you can't just do it any time you like. And without theory, no practice. I have the book in my pocket, because I know myself, because questions have kept popping up in the last few days. Braking distance? Reaction time? Take another look at the formula and, yes, I know, reaction time plus braking distance is stopping time. If I didn't know that by now, I'd be thick as two planks. All you have to do is look at the thicks that are with me in the driving school, who can't grasp the simplest rule of three. Complete idiots are driving around in cars, kept back at school a hundred times but have a driving licence.

But because I know myself, that before tests I always need to keep mugging up, because otherwise I go mad. So, book in hand, dog in hand, newspapers in hand, keys in hand, yes, and the crap bags too, though Bonnie doesn't want to do a crap at all today, and she's peed already, so now it's all about sniffing.

And there's no rush either, because I don't have to get to the bakery like on other days. Can have a nice breakfast after this, have a leisurely shower, have a cup of coffee, have another one. It's a bit loopy, though, to be sitting around waiting for it to be nine o'clock, at work I'd at least be distracted. I'll drive myself mad at home. Level crossing? Parking in front of a level crossing sign?

Of-bloody-course I can do it.

That would be ridiculous!

And walking along the street, suddenly there's a rustling in a front garden and Bonnie stops. Rooted to the spot. Won't budge, because there's this rustling, it's so exciting that something is rustling – Bonnie's life is very boring. 'Bonnie, come on.' Not a budge.

Rustle-rustle. 'Bonnie, it's just a bunny, come on.'

But then the bunny curses.

And I don't need to be an expert to know that bunnies don't curse. OK, so that is exciting. So I stop too and listen. Is it a burglar? Should I call the police, maybe? But burglars don't curse, do they? No. Doesn't really sound like a burglar either. I move on a few metres, to see if I can get a better view of what is going on behind that bush. Bonnie yelps quietly, really just a 'woof', followed by a bit of growling. Another step to the side. Bonnie woofs again, then Jana turns around, 'Shshsh!'

'Listen,' I say, but she only goes 'Shshsh' again, louder this time.

Jana is standing by a window on the ground floor and is struggling, trying to climb in.

I stand and stare. Bonnie wags her tail and pulls me towards Jana, gives another soft little woof. Pants.

'Shshshshsh!' out of Jana.

'Hey, look here,' I say.

Jana sighs, turns around and rustles to us through the shrubbery.

'Give me a hand,' she says.

'What with?' I ask stupidly.

'I can't get into my bedroom.'

'Use the door! Look, there's this opening in the house, it's there for that actual purpose. Brilliant or what?'

'I can't go in the door!' She rounds on me.

'Well that's too bad. Looks like you're going to have to sleep in the garden, doesn't it?'

'What did I ever do to you?'

'How do you mean? I'm just going by with my dog delivering the newspaper.'

'Look, will you help me? Give us a leg up, please?'

'Tell me, how old are you?'

'Fifteen.'

'Stop messing me about.'

'Fourteen.'

'Rubbish!'

'Look, that is beside the point. Are you going to help me or not?'

'You're making a bit of a habit of crossing my path.'

'I live here! You're walking past!'

Jana bends down to Bonnie and pats her.

'All right, then, let's get on with it. I have other things to do.'

We go to the house, I take a look at it all up close, say, 'You can't get up there? That's ridiculous.'

'I have weak arms.'

'Then maybe in future you shouldn't climb out of the window at night.'

'Yes, Mummy.'

I hold my hands out, she climbs up, I give a bit of a heave and she's on the windowsill, almost falls into the room, curses softly but doesn't actually fall. Jana turns around to me, says 'Thanks' quickly. Then she closes the window and draws the curtains. Bonnie gives another soft woof, looks at me, gives a quizzical wag, and because nothing else happens, I walk on, deliver the rest of the papers, go home, kill time, and at nine I go to the driving school, and fail my theory test.

FAILING

There's this one question, it's just like it used to be with dictation in primary school. After we'd done those, I always knew, by the time break came round, which word I had got wrong, and I'd ask the others, because I knew there was something not quite right with that particular word. And it always was wrong. And I come out of the test, thinking, Mmm, that question, the one about … that should have been … and when the next person comes out and sits down on the steps near the entrance, and I've never spoken to him before, but I talk to him now, ask him if he could just tell me, and he's: 'Ah, nah, haven't a clue.' And lights a cigarette. And then she comes out, and she's got her driving test immediately, oh, you can't talk to her. Says: 'Well, even if I've failed, at least I've got some free time, my boss isn't expecting me till two.' I'd like to say something as well, like, yes, I've got a boss too, but as far as they are concerned I'm just a stupid idiot, the way they are looking at me. Well, I've never exchanged a word with them, I suppose I can't suddenly expect great solidarity. Nothing for it but to wait. The others smoke. I don't smoke, because I don't smoke. At last it's time, and everyone has handed in their papers.

It's not as if it was hard to mark. They have this model set of answers that they check your paper against, they just have to look and tick things off, and that's it. And they do that for

… thirteen people … oh, thirteen, not a good number. And then Kehrer comes out too and looks, and the one who has her driving test right away says, 'Well?' practically shouts it.

He nods at her, tells her to get ready.

'Unfortunately, not everyone has passed this time,' he says, and I think, Oh well, I'll have passed anyway.

It was ridiculous. I know how many mistakes I'm allowed, and if there's a tick against this one question, then I'm home and dry.

Then he comes to me and says, 'Lord, girl, that thing about braking distance …' I'm thinking, what about braking distance? What's he going on about braking distance for? And he asks a question, which I answer, and he says, 'Yes, that's right, it must have been the tension, huh?'

I don't get it.

Then he says, 'Well, next time then, in two weeks.'

What's in two weeks?

The test.

What test? The practical? In two weeks?

But the way he's looking at me, I think, no-o-o, the theory.

I. Have. Failed.

I've failed, and I check my watch, best get back to work then. In two weeks. I've failed.

And then I'm outside the Corner Bakery, it's so bloody hot here again. A fan at the threshold, another in the cubbyhole, both stirring warm air around, but it doesn't help. And Angela says: 'Lord, the boss has just been. So? Did it go well?'

'What did he want?'

'What?'

'The boss? What did he want?'

'Forgotten something. But, listen, how did it go? Hard? I sweated blood when I did it. But I'm not good at tests,' says Angela. Fanning herself. 'It feels as if it's getting warmer all the time.'

'It's going to be 39 degrees tomorrow,' I say.

'That's not normal. Maybe we should get time off because of the heat.'

Angela looks out of the window.

'And when have you the practical?' she suddenly says.

I shrug.

'Before the holidays are over?'

'I never failed anything before. Is there any coffee left?'

I go into the cubbyhole behind.

We've started to put a jug of coffee into the fridge to chill it, add cold milk to it. Half a cup of coffee, half of milk, add a cube of ice.

I go back to Angela. There's a customer, then another one comes in, and off we go, it's soon lunchtime, time flies.

I've never failed before. I never got an E. Once in my life I got a D but that was only because I'd been sick. I can do maths, I can remember dates, I can remember everything that I want and need to remember, formulas, poems, names, vocabulary. I've never failed before. He said I'd failed. No, maybe I misunderstood, and he didn't mean me at all.

It can't be. I am not a person who fails. And the baguettes are sold out. Will we be getting any more today, someone asks, she wants them for a barbecue this evening. So I ring the boss and he says yes, no, says, 'Yes, no, well, how many does she want?' Ten baguettes. OK, he'll do it, she should come back at four, well, and how did the test go, he asks. Hard?

It wasn't hard, though. I've done harder tests. I've done tests in Latin, those were harder, this was multiple-choice. How could I have failed? I'm not stupid. I learnt the stuff. I got my sleep, I ate properly, I don't take drugs, I don't even smoke! So I say, 'I failed,' hang up and say, 'Yes, can I help you?'

'Oh, no, Louise, failed?' says Angela.

I make a gesture, keep looking at the customer, 'Yes?'

'Oh, dear, failed?' she asks.

'She had her theory test today,' says Angela, starts serving the customer herself.

'Ach! My son had to do every test three times! He only ever got through on the third attempt.'

Yes, but your son is probably a right thick, but you don't know that, because you're far too fond of him. Your son can fail five tests as far as I am concerned, but me! I! Do! Not! Fail!

Jana

INTENSIVE. CARE. UNIT.

They had an item on the radio today, ideas about the best places to be in this heat. In the cinema, in the supermarket, in the museum, that kind of thing. Because it's so warm again, or rather, not warm, but really hot. Mum has left the shutters down everywhere, and I'm not supposed to open any windows in case the warm air from outside comes in.

But it's warm here all the same.

And it's unbearable in the garden. The trees aren't trees at all, they're too small still. And the neighbour had his cut back last year. Not as much as a breath of air. And because it is so hot and even though it is so hot, I go out. Wearing a hat. A big straw hat it has such a wide brim I might as well be dragging my own private parasol around.

I get myself a lemonade at the kiosk, but it's all gone after two blocks. I'm drinking myself silly in this heat. So I go to the supermarket and buy myself a big bottle of water. But I haven't brought a bag, that's stupid.

So then I'm standing at the checkout wondering if I should get myself some chewing gum, like a little air conditioner in your mouth, and what kind of chewing gum tastes coldest.

The one in the blue packet for sure. Anything with mint in it.

And then it's my turn and I haven't taken any chewing gum, so I pay just for the water and I turn around and fumble the change into my back pocket. Someone calls me, someone who's at the other checkout. Mia, with someone or alone, and she comes over to me really quickly and I'm still there, wasn't fast enough to run away.

And then she's standing there, looking sadly at me, and she's not even my friend, but she is in my class. And And she's sooo … Why? Because Mia was sweet on Tom when he jumped/fell/landed. And because Tom spoke three sentences to her once.

Something like, 'Do you know what time the bus is at?' or 'So is Steinke still sick?' or 'Jana is in your class, isn't she, could you give her this please?' and not 'Mia, I think you're wonderful, would you like to be my girlfriend?' or 'Mia, I've only just noticed you today! How could I go through life without appreciating you and your beauty? From now on, every day that I must spend without you will be torment.' And not even 'Like to snog?'

Not even that.

Mia is on the verge of tears. Three sentences, and now she's about to cry.

'Hey,' says Mia.

'Yes?' I say.

'So how are you?' she asks. And not the way people ask, 'So, everything good with you?' but 'And how are YOU?' emphasis on YOU.

Because SHE is suffering.

'Good. You too?'

Now she looks away briefly, takes far too deep a breath, in and out.

Then looks at me, deep into my eyes.

'Not good. I put up a page. For me and Tom. So that I can somehow come to terms with it.' Pause. 'How ... is he?'

I shrug my shoulders.

Mia doesn't go to the hospital. Because she couldn't bear it, she says.

'I'm going there now. Would you like to come with me?' I say far too fast and think, Oh, shit, suppose she really does come with me?

But I'm in luck, because Mia says that she can't do that yet, that she's not strong enough for that.

Aha.

Right, so I'm off, then.

'I'll send you the link,' she says, and I say bye and I really don't know what she's talking about.

And so that I won't have been lying, I do really go to the hospital. And the hospital is also one of those places where it is not so hot, a place where it is nearly bearable, at least from the point of view of the temperature.

Tom is not in a single room. They said that it might even be better for him in that condition (in HIS CONDITION) not to be alone. There's someone in the next bed, who has been lying there like Tom, only much longer. So long that the whole wall by his bed is full of pictures and postcards, there's even an MP3 player with earbuds, and there are things all over the place to remind him.

He jumped too. Or fell. From the fourth floor, landed on the ground. And here.

And there's someone here who often comes. A woman with cherry-red lips and black hair, she looks like Snow White, so beautiful, she looks like winter. And she has his hand in her hand again and she says nothing. Sits there, has an earbud in her ear, has stuck the other earbud in his ear. It's very soft, I can't even hear it. She's looking at him. And sometimes she gives a quick smile, so quickly that it is nearly gone before I've had a chance to see it. And then she sits there with his hand in hers and two ears together and with a song and a cable between them.

And because I don't want to be staring at her, I only nodded briefly when I came in, said hello softly. Here it's nearly always as quiet as this, except when Mum and Dad are here, but they are way too loud. As if Tom is hard of hearing. Like before, when he didn't want to go to school, and they always called/ yelled at him to get up in the morning. He had to get up eventually. Now he can stay in bed as long as he likes, it's the holidays after all.

I open the water bottle as quietly as possible. I turn the top very slowly, and it hisses, and my hand gets a bit wet, but I do it so slowly that it doesn't fizz up, it only hisses, fresh and cold, and I get even thirstier.

I haven't even looked again at the picture that hangs at the entrance, when you arrive at the unit here. At first I took it for a child's drawing, but then thought that it's too good to be by a child but at the same time it's sketchy and looks as if it was drawn with a black felt pen on paper. And Dad saw it too at some point and shook his head, said: 'How could they?' But he wasn't asking anyone how they could, how they could hang this picture here with the big man on the unravelling horse and the little round man with a hat on the bunny/stag/squirrel that was supposed to be a donkey. And the crosses that don't turn. Windmills.

And you can't just say, 'Art' or something, because Dad has shaken his head and said, how could they?

So I always give it a look when I go past it and think of Dad's head.

Only not today.

And drink, and close the bottle again and have it securely

in my hands, and near my stomach, my chest, a litre and a half of cooling.

How she sits there.

And then I push the chair closer and look at Tom. Tom's lips are quite dry, there's a white scum on his mouth, which nobody has wiped away. And no tongue to lick it quickly away. No-one to say, Tom, you've got something there, so that he opens his eyes and says: 'Where?' And the funny thing is that people always start wiping in the wrong place and then in the right place and if you say, yes, it's gone, they still give it another wipe to be absolutely sure.

Snow White can't see me any more now, the way I am bent over Tom.

'Tom, you have something there on your lip,' I say. And he doesn't wipe it and doesn't ask, 'Where?' and doesn't wipe/lick in the wrong place and doesn't wipe again.

And there are crumbs of sleep in his eyes. Sleep dust. Dream powder.

I get rid of it. Very carefully. And then I root my lip balm out of my pocket and smear it over his lips, so they don't chap. He doesn't notice. No problem. So. And then I give a little laugh, because I think of Mia, and I think how funny Tom might find it, that he would maybe laugh, that he would joke with me the way we did when we were small. Or maybe he might get angry, maybe with Mia, say, what is she thinking of, that chick, that bimbo? But maybe Tom wouldn't use words like 'chick' or 'bimbo', maybe it would be me he'd be angry with, because he finds Mia not bad, because he thinks, ah, that's nice, that she's sad and that it's not something to be laughing stupidly about, that I am the chick, the bimbo, the stupid thing.

And nothing else occurs to me. Those two over there, they have at least a few songs, two earbuds and a cable between them.

And because nothing-nothing-nothing occurs to me that I could say or do, because I don't know if Tom would laugh about Mia, that's why I leave very quickly. And quicker. And I am angry with him, because maybe he's cross with me, because I'm mean about Mia, find her silly and irritating, because I would like to smack Mia one, she doesn't know Tom at all. But neither do I and I leave and I'm out and the picture is only on a hook and Dad won't need to shake his head any more if he comes later.

HOW IT STARTED

maybe can't be said at all after the event, but when – that I
do know, because I wondered, because it was just before the
holidays. It was the kind of day when everyone is a bit more
relaxed because the teachers aren't going to spring a test on
us at this stage, because there's no homework, because we just
have to put in a few more hours before we can all go home,
because it's Shrove Tuesday, carnival. And it was really just like
always, he sat beside me, just like he did all year round, because
we'd agreed that during the summer holidays. Because we were
friends, because I wanted to help him to get through the year,
not to have to stay back again. So he sat beside me, and I'd
given up my place at the window for him, because Constanze
and Janina didn't want to sit beside him. And so it went for a
few months, and all was well, he was managing, I explained
maths to him, we were friends, sometimes he distracted me,
but nothing I couldn't cope with. And no, it wasn't love, on
either side, and you could say that it had to do with one heart
or the other, or with pride or stubbornness, or with revenge
or being unfulfilled or something like that, sometimes the

wind just changes. And I thought, it's just that his girlfriend something or other or his parents, that's why he came in this particular day and didn't say hello to me. Thought, he's just in a bad mood, maybe I made a joke, and maybe it was the joke, or maybe not. But anyway, for the first time, Paul said something to me that felt like a punch in the stomach. And I knew he was capable of that. But to me he'd never done anything like that. But there you go. And the ones in front of us heard it, the ones behind us as well, Constanze, Janina. And because everyone was a little bit afraid of him, everyone held their tongues, before the first person let out a laugh.

And maybe now you could say that at that point, I should have said something, something like THUS-FAR-AND-NO-FURTHER or NO-THAT'S-NOT-ON. And if it was one of those stories from which we are all supposed to emerge a bit smarter and a bit bigger, then someone would have stood up bravely in front of me and would have shown courage and said to him that he should be careful what he says, and who he says it to. But nobody had the backbone. Not in my class. Nobody had the nerve to say anything, and if there had been someone, then it would be me, I'd be the one to do it. And I didn't do it. And if you let it go, because you think that after the holidays it will all go back to the way it was before, then it can easily happen that attacks like this happen again. And at some stage, there are kicks under the table as well as digs. And a cola that he accidentally-on-purpose poured into my bag. And before long the others are laughing much more readily, and suddenly the wind changes. And people think, oh well, it'll change back again. And the teacher says: 'Louise and Paul, quiet now' because I've kicked back under the table. And the teacher thinks no more about it, nor the next teacher either. And that the two there in the third row are constantly making trouble, you just have to intervene quickly, verbally, just take heed, communicate, and then all is well. And then the next lesson comes along. And he still needs help in maths, but it's not worth it any more. And he whispers so loudly that you can hear it, whispers: 'Stupid, but useful.'

And when he's gone, because he is sick, or playing sick, then you can see what a vacuum is left behind him, so that everyone is asking if maybe he is coming around the corner, so that they can see him again. But then because he doesn't appear suddenly, they don't look any more. And then it's Louise again. And not Paul.

You still get invited to parties, but there comes a point where you really don't want to go any more, you'd rather read a book or watch a DVD or study something. Only Constanze's laugh was not loud. Janina didn't care, you could never rely on her anyway. But every time he hit home, there was never a word out of Constanze, and she kept quiet, even when the others laughed.

Things didn't improve. There were quiet days, there were

hellish days. And there came a day when I didn't sit in my place any more, but in the back row. But moving away is not just some kind of a consequence. Paul banishes Louise. Everyone saw, you couldn't avoid it, and one teacher thought it was just some teenage split-up melodrama, but he didn't take it any further because it didn't look like developing into a real incident. So there I stayed and at some stage they just gave up looking towards the back. Constanze moved up a place. Janina too. Nobody asked me back. I didn't explain maths to him any more, but he managed it somehow. I have no idea how.

And once I did go to a party. And he was there and there were others there too. I danced until I was aching all over, and then I saw Paul and Constanze lying in a corner, snogging. And so she had a boyfriend and he a girlfriend. But that explains nothing, or maybe just a bit, and on the following Monday, they were all saying that I had been snogging someone from one of the other classes in our year. But what was going on between Constanze and Paul, nobody mentioned that. And at the end of the day, there's only yourself. If a party used to be cool before only if you had been there yourself, somehow that has changed, and now the phone doesn't ring any more after lunch, and the weekends are free, and at break you can read a book. You have time and nobody needs you. And that's not so bad.

That you can survive.

EXCUSES

Constanze had been watching me the whole time. And I do notice a thing like that, if someone is watching me all the time, stares like that. But because it's lunchtime and everyone has to buy bread and sandwiches and such, it's busy at the Corner Bakery. Like every day at this time, even in the heat, when you'd expect the people to be at the lake or sitting around in air-conditioned rooms and not here. Before it is Constanze's turn, there's someone who wants a walnut loaf, two Kaiser rolls, muffins, a chocolate roll, a Frankfurt cake, a wholemeal baguette, a cheese baguette, a puff pastry pig's ear, a pound of coffee, a cup of coffee and an advance order, and then she is in front of me. Although she could just as easily order from Angela. But no, there she stands and doesn't say, 'Good afternoon,' but, 'Hello'.

And I don't say, 'What can I do for you?' either but, 'Hi.'

And Angela doesn't even look up, because the next person has come up and is ordering something from her. Behind Constanze are the builders from Leibnizstraße, one of whom Angela likes, and she makes to serve him. And Constanze stands there and looks, and I'm thinking she's going to have to say what she wants at some stage.

'Didn't know you were working here.'

What can you say to that? 'Really, didn't you?' or 'Well, I

never told you, when could I have done that?'

So I just shrug my shoulders and do something with my face. And she's: 'Been doing it long?'

'Three weeks.'

'Well?'

Well what?

Shrugs again.

We used to laugh at this kind of granny small-talk. There was a time when we made a joke of it, we called each other by our surnames, pretended we had hats on and handbags at our elbows and rabbited on about the excellent weather. I look behind her. There's Mrs Doctor So-and-so, who's only called that because her husband is a doctor. And because nobody, including herself, understands that she is not automatically entitled to be called doctor because of that. And Mrs Doctor always wants the same thing, I could easily have laid it all out myself, but I did that once and she got peevish, and ordered something different on purpose. And she is impatient, because Mrs Doctor is on a rigid timetable, which she sticks to, regardless of the heat. And so she is also looking.

Then eventually: 'I'm supposed to buy bread. Eh, rye mix.'

I point to the bread, Constanze nods, I wrap it up, and then, force of habit, 'Can I get you anything else?' and before we'd have had a laugh about that, but it was different then. Now she says: 'That's all.' And gives me money and I give her change and I'm looking behind her already, and then she says: 'Listen, if you have time …'

And I answer: 'I'm pretty busy right now,' and I might be referring to the people who are waiting and want to buy something, or I might be referring to my holidays, or I might just mean 'No,' and she leaves. Mrs Doctor wants the same as usual and I think, 'You stupid, predictable cow.' Check my watch, I have another hour and a half to go. Mrs Doctor is niggling at me now, so subtle, in a way very stupid people might think she means it kindly, but I'm too common for that, even if I have a better school certificate than she has, even if I will not be called Mrs Doctor in the future just because my husband is a doctor. But now I am standing behind the counter and must serve her, as she is accustomed to, because she comes from the kind of family where people are always served, which used to be called, and which no doubt she still calls, being from a good family. And what is going on with Constanze anyway that she suddenly wants to talk to me? Seems as if she's bored. Has she nothing better to be doing? Hasn't she got a boyfriend to cheat on, can she not hang around some lake or other and get herself sunburnt? Couldn't she just change schools, like him? Did she not want to? Did he not take her with him?

And then I cut my hand as I am trying to halve a loaf, deep, it's bleeding, and great excitement. I should run it under the tap first off, but on the other hand, that's exactly what you are not supposed to do, I should go behind, before I get blood on everything, and then someone says: 'Oh, that looks bad, she should really get a doctor to look at it. Lord, Louise, what are you going to do?'

I look up and I'm looking the kid in the eye.

Angela says: 'Oh, you know each other?'

Jana nods and then she starts lying again like mad, says she's my cousin, that she's locked herself out and has really just come by to ask me for our key, because we have a spare key. And now this. And says I've always had such a low blood count and had to take iron.

'Oh, my, you're white as a sheet,' she says and Angela gets nervous.

'Louise, maybe you should go home.' Then she turns to Jana. 'You'll take her, won't you?'

Jana nods so sincerely that I nearly laugh out loud. But my hand hurts too much, even if the cut is not so deep that it needs to be seen by a doctor. But Angela doesn't need to know that. I am suffering a bit, Jana is a bit fretful and Angela promises not to say a word to the boss, and I can have the rest of the day off and a tea-towel as a bandage.

Three blocks later, Jana stops and looks at the hand. 'Leave it,' I say.

'I only want to look.'

'It's not too bad.'

'You don't know that.'

'In the first place, it is MY hand, and in the second place, I live right beside the hospital, they know there what's bad and what isn't.'

'Right.'

Jana lets my hand go and walks on. At some point she stops and says: 'Well then …'

And me: 'What do you mean, well then? You're supposed to be taking me home. I am badly injured.'

'Not annoying you, am I?'

I shrug my shoulders. I still have to go out with the dog and do more test papers and then in the evening I have to go to the driving school, so that I might just learn something, and then another round with the dog and then early to bed and the out again early and then I think of Constanze, all she has to do is go to the shop for rye mix bread.

'I just need to go home for a while,' I say.

When we reach the front door, Jana looks around as if someone is following her.

'Is something wrong?' I ask.

'Nah,' she says.

I look, but there's nobody, nothing. Only Jana is suddenly different.

Smaller.

Jana

DAZED

I'm thinking that Mum will be leaving the office soon and going to the hospital and that she always comes this way, if she sees me here … But Louise is already opening the door, going quickly inside. She puts her index finger to her lips, but she doesn't need to do that at all, it's so weirdly quiet here that you go all quiet yourself. And then I see a man lying on the sofa, it must be her father, and she opens a door and looks into the bedroom, where there is a woman lying on the bed. She closes the door again, takes the lead and I ask her quietly: 'How come your parents are sleeping?'

'Because they are tired.'

Maybe her parents are sick. But why are they sleeping with their clothes on? And why not in the same room? I find that all very strange, and there's a note, just like at home, and I didn't check this morning what was on mine. And I'll get an earful later, or maybe not. And then here comes the dog, who has to keep quite also, but the lead is clinking against its collar, and we get out of there fast.

I let my breath out. Then I think of Mum again.

I have to get out of here.

'Are you coming?' asks Louise.

I want to know where we are going, but it doesn't really matter, I only want to get out of here and hope that Louise will take a route where we won't meet Mum coming towards us. And the good thing is, that is exactly what she does. Shortcut. Shortcut where cars aren't allowed. That's good.

So I give up watching and I haven't a clue where we are, but that's good too, because if this is a place I don't know, then Mum won't come driving along here either. And now we're at a house that I don't know, but Louise does, and so does the dog. And Louise even has the key. As we stand there at the door, a neighbour looks out of the window, all nosy. Louise waves at her, mentions her name, and says that her granny had rung her and then she says a few more things, so the woman stops making herself out to be so important and eventually her head disappears back into the house.

Louise opens up and in runs the dog.

It smells of granny and it looks like that too. If I ask what we're doing here, then Louise will definitely bawl me out again and send me packing. But I don't want to go, I want to stay with Louise and the dog, even if it smells of granny here.

She just goes in and says: 'Close the door,' so I close the front door, stand in the hall and wait.

It's a strange house, I don't know my way around, I stand

and wait and then she comes back and she has a bag and she has the dog with her again and the door opens again and Louise says, 'Come on.'

Nobody is expecting me at home, and I've already been to the hospital. There's a picture missing there now, I took it out of its frame, folded it up small and stuck it in my pocket, put the frame on a wall on the road, someone will have taken it by now.

And they will say, yes, Jana's been, and Mum and Dad can sit there together and be told something, medical data, and when or whether Tom can be patched-up/mended/operated-on.

'Come on,' says Louise again and holds the door open, so out I go, come on where, though?

Louise closes the door, locks up, the dog wags its tail, Louise has sunglasses on and goes in front of me, round the house, crunch of gravel. She rattles a key, opens a car door, gets in and opens the door for me from the inside, because it's an old car.

The car is small and also smells of granny and air freshener. The car is so old that it has a radio with a thing for cassettes and there are also cassettes lined up. I don't want to listen to them, but maybe we're just going to do the shopping or something.

And Louise turns on the engine: 'Well, what do you know, it works.' And then off we go and she looks out for the neighbour, but she can't see us from her house, she'd have to come out, and it's too hot for that. And the car is so old that it has no air conditioning, so Louise opens her window and so do I and the dog lies there in the back, and there's a draught because the car is moving.

'May I?' I ask. Louise looks at me and I'm pointing to the radio and she nods. I turn the radio on and it's only talk and a bit of classical music and then more talk. A lot of people have died somewhere and I'm looking for a different station. And then a good song and when the song is over someone is talking again, but in English.

I close my eyes and the breeze whispers around me and fingers my hair. Sometimes it's not bad to be quiet. There is a kind of silence that is bad, gets under your skin and makes your eyes water. And then there's a kind of silence that is like lying in a meadow with bumble-bees. Or driving along with a dog behind me and wind in my hair and English talk on the radio that goes so fast you can hardly hear the bad news.

Then I open my eyes again and we are somewhere completely different. Not in the city any more, that was quick.

And look over there and maybe I should ask: 'So where are we going?'

'Haven't a clue.' Louise giggles. 'Is that a problem? Have you got an appointment?'

'Nah,' I say.

'Will anyone miss you?'

I'm fumbling with the volume control until it's all just as loud as it was before.

'If you need to go to the loo or you're hungry or whatever, just let me know, OK? Or if you want to get out? All right?'

'OK.'

I look out the window, then at her.

'And your hand?'

'It's fine, doesn't hurt any more. Look,' she says and takes her hand off the steering wheel for a moment. 'If you live beside the hospital you can do ace bandaging.'

And then I realise that she did all that while I was standing around in the hall and with only one hand. She doesn't need anyone.

She asks: 'Have your parents got a car?'

'Two,' I say.

'Ah, two. So they drive a lot?'

'Yeah, think so.'

'And you go with them a lot of the time, right?'

'Yes?'

'Then tell me, since you're sitting there beside me, how am I doing at the driving?'

'OK.'

'OK. Good. OK is good, right?'

I shrug my shoulders.

'OK means you are not afraid I'm about to have an accident?'

'Yes. Yeah, I'm not afraid.'

'So I'm a good driver, right?'

'Think so, yeah.'

Louise nods.

And says softly: 'Exactly.'

Then she's quiet for a bit and then she says: 'Tell me, you're not afraid of me at all, are you?'

'What do you mean, afraid?'

'Have your parents not told you that you shouldn't just go off driving with strangers?' she asks, and I think it's a bit late for that now. It's already happened. And go, 'Pff.' And then I say: 'Maybe I do know you. And are you not afraid of me?'

Louise looks over at me and says: 'Nah. You're harmless.' And smiles.

Because she is smiling harmless doesn't sound bad, not babyish, not like 'You haven't a clue' but OK.

And then she looks at me and says 'What'll we do now?' and she's grinning.

'I can decide?'

'Your decision.'

'Could we watch shooting stars?'

'But it's still bright.'

'Then I've decided that it's dark now, night time.'

Louise / Jana

PRETEND

So what are you doing for the holidays? Are you going to the south of Europe? With your parents, friends? Have you got a job? Are you doing work experience? Do you want to spend lots of time at the lake/at the pool/with your friend? Are you just going to fritter the time away or have you made plans or are you all planned out, organised?

Do something different. Nick your granny's car, which isn't really stealing because she won't know a thing about it, because she is in Tuscany and because nicking things belonging to your family doesn't count as stealing. Leave your job, let the others stew, and leave your brother there in the hospital. Forget the last year at school and that your parents don't talk to each other any more. And if you feel like it, change your name, don't call yourself Louise any more or Lou, Lulu, Louisie, you could be an Indian, the daughter of a chief. You can be anything you want in the summer, you can try a foreign language or invent one. The summer has a thousand and one doors. And they're all ajar, because it's so hot. Your parents have to work and worry about the carpet getting dusty or the flowers dying of thirst, your parents have tax returns to do and insurance companies to change, referrals to make, your parents have to make pension provisions and have medicals to attend.

You don't even have to vote!

So it's night and it's dark. When you were a child, that worked, you said it, look, I've found money, hundreds and thousands and millions of euro, and we are going to eat as much ice-cream as we want. And if it is night and shooting stars fall, then you can make a wish and every wish will come true, EVERY BLOODY WISH. So make as many wishes as you can think of, and then Jana and Louise or Josie and Louana travel on with the dog, me an you and a dog named Boo (short for Bonnie). Strawberry ice-cream then. And a drink from the filling station. Seriously, though, you look eighteen, as long as you don't do anything stupid, if you just drive up in your car and behave as if the kid beside you is your sister, you could even buy hard liquor at the petrol station. Especially since you're driving a car, and who is going to ask if you have or haven't got a driving licence? Not! A! Soul! When we used to be on holidays, even the little boys would be scooting around on mopeds and you have done nearly all your driving lessons, so there is absolutely nothing to worry about. And if you want cigarettes, then just buy some or ask your older sister who doesn't look a bit like you to buy some. So what next? 'Now we're going to the lake, to the lake, now we're going to the lake.

With a wooden root, root-root-root.' Giggling. Music louder. Is that Italy already or still Hessen? Have we just been going round in circles?

Do you really let your parents tell you what you should do in the holidays? Just because they always had to work, and had to walk to school in ten metres of snow in cardboard shoes and nothing to eat either in those days, or in general, rubbish. We can sleep when we're dead, work if we have to. Come on, we're mermaids and we're diving. I can stand on my hands. I can do the forward roll, Lou, Lou, skip to my Lou, backwards, sideways, and skip to my Lou my darling! If it is too hot, then we'll just do a rain dance. And buttermilk after swimming, because that's the best thing after swimming. So maybe the lake is only an outdoor pool and now you smell and taste of chlorine, but there's buttermilk, good, swimming pools smell like freshly mown lawns, of sun-cream and chips. The fat child has been on the one-metre board since morning, practising cannon-balling, and doesn't splash the woman on the edge of the pool until after one. We don't want views of the sights, but postcards with parrots on them. And we write some, write 'Dear friend, greetings from the Socio-economic Republic of Snuffistan. Weather super, but the lemonade is not good. Have learnt songs and in future will do more for the general well being of my community, more ribbons on trees! Pink! Your friend, Daniela!' and send them to your primary school teacher.

And if anyone asks, we are on our way, we're just out to get milk, we're on the way to Grandmother's, who is sick in bed, with cake, bread and wine and ask: 'Are you the big bad wolf?'

And laugh like nobody has ever laughed before. Three hundred kinds of laughter. Giggling is in a separate category.

Let's get a bit of air.

And close our eyes.

Take care that you don't get sunburnt. I fell asleep once in the sun.

And then?

And then … we'll do something different.

What would you like to do?

We are a two-headed monster, and when you're grown up, when I'm grown up, then you'll teach me how to drive. Now there are two arms at the steering wheel, one head is looking at the road, the other one can swerve. We have another pair of hands, which can get out the snacks and change the radio station. Then we put Cliff Richard on and laugh a bit.

So where are we going? Two heads and no compass, no compromise, you say Greece, I say Greenland, you say Molokai, I say Mongolia. Maybe we can agree at least about a letter, B, B is a good letter, places beginning with B are Bangladesh, Bayreuth and Beirut.

Berlin and Benin. That won't do, we won't travel another metre, I say, let's rest and stretch our legs, and you laugh, giggle, your cheeks are red. We're not exactly spitting fire and we're going around in circles. We've been on the road a month, a year, and only a few hours. We could tell you something different, you'd have to believe us. I tell you we were on safari and when tigers and lions have babies they are called Liger and Tion. That's daft, but it can't be helped. No, you say, they can't meet each other at all in the wild. So we tell you that we've been to the South Pole, we wanted to see penguins. Why, you ask, because there are other animals if you go somewhere else, pandas or koalas, duck-billed platypuses, butterflies as big as dinner plates. We're driving through California and stop at a filling station, we order a coffee, brown water, and the woman asks us where we've come from and we say Germany and she says, 'All the way by car?' All right, so that didn't actually happen to us but to someone else.

You fold your arms, say, well, so, then? What really happened?

Well, all right.

Jana

FOR REAL

Louise says that I am the one to decide. I've never done that. So there had to be shooting stars because I have never seen any before and made a wish.

But it is still daytime, no matter how hard I decide that it's night, even if we put on our sunglasses. Louise says she needs to get petrol, so we go to a filling station and the dog can get out, gets water and does a bit of sniffing. She fills up, and I just stand there. Then we go in to pay and she turns to me and says: 'We need supplies!' So we grab what we can, chocolate and ice-cream and sandwiches, lots of drinks and also a cold beer. 'Anything else?' she asks, and I think maybe I'd like to smoke tonight? Do I want to? I don't know. Better not. Then we pay and pick up our stuff and get back in the car.

'Where to?' she asks.

I can't think of anything. It's still light. 'Swimming?' I ask. 'Lake or pool?'

And because I haven't got any proper swimming gear with me, I say lake, and Louise starts singing. And it's really funny. 'But why root?' I ask. 'And why wooden?'

'Because back when the song was written, roots were mostly made of cardboard, and if you used them for rowing, then they would just go all soggy. So you had to ask specifically for a wooden root. In case someone tried that and sank in the lake. But they don't make roots out of cardboard any more.' Then she sticks out her hand and that means I'm supposed to give her the water bottle so that she can have a drink and I've finished my ice-cream. 'And anyway with a cardboard root doesn't sound so good.'

'True.'

'Yes, they really did think about what they were doing when they were writing that song.'

So then we sing some more: We're going to the lake, to the lake, we're going to the lake! Louder than the radio. The dog starts yowling and we're laughing.

'Bonnie! You're singing!' says Louise, looking in the rear-view mirror.

And then we drive and get to the lake and it's not one I know but Louise does and it's lovely here with a tree and not a soul about, only us two souls and a doggy soul. So it's no problem to jump into the water in your underwear and I don't need to be embarrassed because my top and my bottom don't match or that there's a washed-out Kermit on my pants.

And the dog jumps with us into the water and barks and is having a great time and is called Bonnie, and that is a good name for a dog.

So then I say: 'Come on, let's play mermaids!' and then I think, oh, shit, she's going to think that's silly because Lily and Charlotte would definitely find that stupid and would laugh at me. They don't do that kind of thing any more. At some point the others stopped playing. At some point everyone was in love, and had to talk all the time. And I still have the table tennis bat, the cool one, the one Tom wrote 'Magnum 45' on. With a biro. In those days. When he still used to play with me.

So I think, maybe Louise didn't hear that, because she is not laughing at all, but she looks at me and then leaps up and arcs into the water and she does a forward roll. Splashes. When she surfaces she calls over to me: 'So, can you do that?'

Sure I can do that. I can do rolls in the water too. Without getting anything in my nose, I can open my eyes underwater, and stand on my hands and wiggle my toes. We try to stand on each other's shoulders, but that's harder than you might think. And then we sing under water to each other and have to guess what it is.

Then out again and into the shade to catch our breath. And shut our eyes. It's humming, the lake is humming, the tree is humming, the bank is humming. We could stay here till it gets to be autumn.

Then a big cloud comes and stretches over me. The sun is still there and it stays warm, but everything is further away because there's tiredness.

It's still humming, it tickles, something is wafting over me, sniffing at my feet, says: 'No, Bonnie, let her sleep.'

And I want to say I'm not asleep but it's hard.

I try it a few times, but the sentence is so far away, and gone, that I leave it, and maybe I really do fall sleep.

And then I wake up and am hungry. But we were smart, we did the shopping, we eat something. Now it's not quite as bright as it was, I have no idea what time it is, but maybe that doesn't matter.

Bonnie is lying on my leg, looking at a leaf. We jump in to the lake again, this time Bonnie doesn't join us, she waits on the bank for us. Then we're dry, even though we have no towels. Louise sticks blades of grass between her toes, a flower behind her ear, tries to make a daisy-chain. She can't manage it and puts it on my head.

'What a lovely holiday,' says Louise. I nod.

'Dear Granny, The dog is well. Lots of love, Louise,' she says.

'Dear Mum, The kidnappers are not as bad as people think. There are sandwiches. There's also a dog. Don't forget to brush your teeth. Jana.'

'Dear Daddy, please open the window because it's hot. Love, Louise.'

'Dear Charlotte, I'm with the Indians now and have long hair. Longer than you. Going to be a chief. Your friend Jana.'

'Dear Mum, France is boring, so that's why I'm not there. Play nicely with the other children. Love, Louise.'

'Dear Tom,' I say, and then it's not so funny any more, so I throw a stick and say: 'Come on, Bonnie, catch.'

Bonnie looks up when she hears her name, looks in the direction I'm pointing in. Nothing.

'Have you ever been to France?' I ask Louise.

'Only on a school exchange in first year. Not even a week. And you?'

'Yeah.'

'And?' she asks.

I shrug my shoulders.

'So, where was it nice?'

So I try to remember where I was with my parents, with Tom, back then when Tom used to come with us, we went a long way, we were in Africa and Asia and America. We stayed in hotels, with pools. We have videos and photographs.

'I don't know,' I say.

'I like the sea,' I say at some stage.

'Me too,' says Louise. 'I can't bear camping.'

Then she plucks the bits of grass from her toes.

Later Louise gathers up all our rubbish and we leave. There, where we were, there's nothing but flattened grass, so that was that.

And off we go again. I'm dry, she is too, hair and all. I don't want to look at my watch, so I don't. I look at the sky, and it is getting darker, even though we are driving into the sun. Behind us, the night is starting. We drive on and up and on and then stop and engine off and out we get. And there are two blankets in the car and the bag and the dog, all out, all further up. And then sit. Up here. And watch the sun going down, and my face feels like a sunset, orange-red with grey-blue streaks of cloud. All on my cheeks and my forehead. There's chirping and in the corners of the sky it starts to glisten. And glimmer, stars. The sun is sliding down the sky into the crack between the bed and the wall, that's the horizon.

'Are you cold?'

I shake my head.

'Because if you are, take the blanket. I have a jacket in the car.'

And then we drink cola and something like Red Bull, only cheaper, so that we can stay awake, because it will take a while until the sky is dark enough.

'And look, what a piece of luck!' says Louise.

'What?'

'It's a new moon tonight, you can see shooting stars much better.'

'That's not luck,' I say.

'Nah, you're right. You're the decision-maker,' she says.

'Exactly.'

Then we lie on our backs, and even so my eyes are too small

for the sky, even though I have two.

'So, there's the Plough, also called the Big Dipper,' says Louise. 'The Rolls Royce of constellations.'

'And there's the Little Dipper,' I say and point somewhere or other.

'Ah, yes, right. And look, there's the Fridge. Normally, you only see that in winter.'

'And that …' I point. 'That's the Badly Knitted Pullover.'

'Yeah, that's beside the Unwashed Dishes!'

'And there's the Little Koala Bear.'

'That's my favourite.'

Then something flashes in the corner of my eye. I look to the side, don't see any aeroplane, should ask about that. 'That flashing, that's a shooting star, right?'

'You've never seen a shooting star before?'

'No.'

'That's what it'll have been. Sometimes you just see them off to the side. But sometimes they're just like in a picturebook. Just you wait, lots of them will fall tonight. And we still have cola.'

And lying there and looking. And looking. And then the thing with the corner of my eye.

'I hope you're not forgetting to make a wish.'

Oh.

'But don't say what it is!'

And because it's suddenly so hard to say anything, I have to concentrate and think what I want to wish for, so I'm quiet.

And make a wish.

And sometimes wishing is hard. It used to be easier. As a little child, you wish for something like a pony or ice-cream (as much as I can eat and then another three scoops) or for good weather tomorrow so that we can go to the playground. And even a year ago, that I wouldn't be left behind at school, that Charlotte would do more with me than with Lily. That I get bigger boobs or that someone is in love with me.

But that's all so long ago. And those are not the things I want any more, anyone can wish for those things.

But this isn't bad for a start, with the dog lying close to me, all warm. And that someone is playing with me, that there's no smell of hospital here, and there is no list saying hoover.

And then I wish that this will never change. I'd like time just to stop, but if it goes on, then everything should be OK, Tom should be alive and awake and also want to be. And Mum and Dad together again and like each other. And that I exist again.

But shooting stars fall too quickly for wishing that. Sad for a moment, because that's how it is, but then, how does that look, this is enough, isn't it?

It's enough.

And beside me, 'Catch a falling star and put it in your pocket …' I wish I could remember the words, but no star is falling right now and I can't remember. But sometimes it's enough to be with someone who does remember the words, if there's someone who sings on.

Louise

AND THEN WE WAKE UP

And it's cold, damp, because it's still early. It's summer, but there's dew on me. Jana is lying beside me, with her arm around Bonnie.

It's later than usual. I think about the newspapers not being delivered today. I think about how they're going to ring Jonas and then they're going to find out that he's still on holiday, that he's been away the whole time and someone else has been doing the job that he is employed to do. I think about how I should have been in the bakery an hour ago, that I never told anyone I wasn't going to be there.

Bonnie looks up, but she's not looking at me, she's looking towards the car. Because something is ringing there, and it's not my mobile.

As I reach the car, it stops, as I open the door, the ringing starts again, and keeps ringing until I finally find it. I take the mobile and carry it over to Jana, who's still asleep, who doesn't wake up even when it starts ringing again.

'Jana,' I say and poke her gently with my foot. Bonnie growls softly at me. Crazy dog.

'Jana, wake up.'

Something moves under the cover, soft sounds, then it all goes quiet again until I poke her again and even Bonnie is wide awake and jumps up. It takes Jana longer. At some stage, I just put the mobile to her ear, and that works, the mumbling, the mewling gets louder, then she finally wriggles out of the blanket.

'Your mobile,' I say.

'Wha'?'

'Your mobile keeps ringing. Your parents are probably looking for you.'

Jana runs her hands through her hair, rubs her eyes, yawns and stretches.

The mobile goes on ringing.

'Are you not going to answer it?'

Jana looks at her mobile as if she's never seen it before, as if she doesn't know what the thing wants of her.

I'm getting uneasy.

I have to get out of here.

I can still ring work, say I couldn't sleep last night because of the cut, that I only got to sleep an hour ago, say I can't come in today. Something like that. You just have to lay it on thick and they'll believe anything. And the newspapers ... I'll think of something.

I still have the car keys in my hand, I start to jingle them.

'Come on, get up. It's time.'

Jana is still staring at her mobile.

'Jana!' I say.

She looks at me as if she's never seen me before in her life, as if she doesn't know what to make of me. That goes on for a while, then she stands up and her mobile is ringing and ringing.

'So, breakfast first, right?' I say, but she doesn't answer, just follows me. OK, so I've let things get a bit out of hand. But I can put it all right, even the theory exam. I'll ask the guy this evening if I can repeat, and not having turned up today at the bakery isn't the end of the world, they'll hardly throw me out, I've behaved very well so far. Nah, I have it all under control. Just need to eat something, with coffee, take the car back, the dog, and then back on course.

Jana gets in.

'Can't you at least put it on silent?'

Jana says nothing, just looks out of the window for a while, then puts the phone on silent.

'You can always tell your parents you slept over at a friend's house and had the phone on silent.'

Jana nods.

'They're not going to eat your head off,' I say.

Looks out of the window again.

There's a bakery in the next village, where I stop. The croissants are still warm, I buy coffee, the cup is far too hot,

I fold a couple of paper napkins around it. I buy Jana a hot chocolate, she's too young for coffee. And anyway she doesn't need to wake up.

Jana has stayed in the car, she stares ahead when I get back in and put the bag on her lap, giving her my coffee and her drink into her hand. 'Careful, it's hot,' I say, but she's still too sleepy even to manage that.

'You're not exactly a morning person, are you?' I ask. The croissants smell great, she doesn't seem to be interested even in that. God she's hopeless in the morning. Then I look at my watch, half seven.

I stop again, at a sort of bit of a park, there's a bench there, say, 'Come on, breakfast,' and Jana gets out. I take the coffee out of her hand, the bag, take a croissant, tear it.

'Are your parents strict?' I ask.

'What?' she says.

'Are your parents strict?'

She shrugs.

'So you won't have a problem when you get home, will you?'

No reaction.

'You've plenty of practice at telling lies, you'll think of something they'll believe,' I say.

'What do you mean?'

'Don't be like that,' I say.

'Like what?' she says and she's suddenly awake, even

without coffee.

'As if you are always absolutely truthful,' I say, grinning at her.

'Oh,' she says, staring back at me.

'Sorry, I don't … I wasn't being mean. Only meant that you'll think of something that your parents …' I say, but she only goes 'Pff.'

And then she folds her arms.

God am I glad I'm past that stage.

So I let her sulk, I let her ignore the hot chocolate, she can refuse breakfast if she likes, what do I care? So, let's go.

As we come into town, she says, 'Can you drive me somewhere, please?'

'Where do you want to go?' She'd better not ask me to drive her home. Her parents are going to be standing at the door asking questions, that's all I need.

'To the hospital.'

'No, I can't do that,' I say, because that's where I live, and if my parents see me …

'PLEASE!' she says, making me wince.

'Why do you want to go there?'

'My brother's in hospital.'

Her brother is there. Jana has a brother. So what do I say now? I'd better just drive on a bit. If she has something to tell me, she'll tell me.

'My parents are there.'

'Listen, if your brother is in hospital, do you not think, yesterday, you should …' I start.

'And who led me astray?'

'Oh, come off it! It's not as if you were bound hand and foot.'

God, her parents are going to be up the wall, and if they see me, there's going to be hell to pay. What is Jana up to?

'You can't just run away when things get hairy,' I say.

'Who's running?' she says.

'So what's wrong with your brother?' I ask.

'Where've you been this last year at school?' she asks me.

'What?' I say, because I really haven't a clue what she is on about.

What does she mean, this last year? What happened? Do I even know her brother?

So then I stop because there's a traffic light and she leaps out of the car, says quickly, 'I'll walk the rest of the way, thanks, bye,' and she's gone and they're starting to hoot behind me.

It's not far to Gran's house, and the neighbour doesn't seem to be there, maybe she never even noticed that the car was gone. I put it where it always is, checking that I haven't left any rubbish, any crumbs in it, because Gran will be back at the weekend. And I put Bonnie back on the lead and we go home, I give her water, feed her, and then she lies down in my room to sleep, because it has all been so bloody stressful. And I call the bakery and Angela is on duty and she says she thought it must have been something like that, I should get some sleep and did the doctor prescribe some painkillers? I say yes and that it'll definitely be better tomorrow and then I go over to Jonas's place, and the newspapers are not there any more, whoever took them. Well, there's nothing I can do about that, and now I have time, since I don't have to work, because I am supposed to have spent the whole night lying awake with a sore hand. I unwrap it and the cut is ridiculous, nearly healed, nothing to worry about.

So then I take a shower and stuff my threads in the washing machine, which is full now, so I wash the load and I eat another croissant and think, maybe I'll take another look at a theory paper. I get it off the shelf, look to see which ones I haven't done yet, and sit there, and I think, what does she mean?

What happened last year?

Did I miss something?

Did somebody in the year behind me or the year ahead of me have an accident? And should I really be sitting here filling in worksheets and there's a note in the kitchen, it says I should take the bottles in the cellar to the bottle-bank, and that's at least two baskets full. I should do that before lunch, because you're not allowed to make noise then, and if you arrive even a minute after one o'clock, the bottle-bank people say you can't put the bottles in because there's a noise ban. And anyway …

Who could I ask?

So I ring Constanze, and while it's ringing, I check my

watch and it isn't even nine yet.

But her mobile is on and she answers.

'Hey!' she says and she's glad, I can tell, I can hear it in her voice, but that's not what it's about, I don't want to meet her for coffee so that she can cry on my shoulder about what Paul has done or hasn't done.

'Hey, I'm glad you rang,' she says and me: 'Yeah, hi, listen, tell me, do you know this kid, she's called Jana, she's in first year or something.'

'Jana? I don't know any first years. What does she look like?'

So I tell her and she's: 'Wait, would that be Tom's sister?'

'Haven't a clue, who's Tom?' I ask.

'Tom. The guy in fifth year. Him, the one that jumped.'

'How do you mean, jumped?'

'Him, the guy who jumped off the bridge.'

God, how clueless can you be? I mean, how bloody clueless?

Jana

NO WAY BACK, NO WAY FORWARD

And I knew all along, as soon as I saw the mobile, that Mum and Dad have been ringing in turn, knew that from now on, everything will be different. If you know that, then everything is already different, but not totally, not yet, not as if someone had actually said it out loud. And I knew, as long as I didn't answer it, it could still be before, before everything just starts to be different. And that's why I get out at the traffic lights, that's why I don't want Louise to drive me to the hospital, I want to walk for a bit, just a few old steps, before the new regime starts. And the whole time, the mobile is ringing. And the news that I haven't read, from Mum, from Dad, from my voicemail. I round a few corners and then I stop. It's getting warm already, and it's a new day. Yesterday was good, yesterday is still good. And maybe I should have known because as soon as it is good, then it gets bad, really bad.

People should be careful of good times, go into hiding until they have gone by, because then maybe the good times would take the bad stuff with them, like the news that Tom jumped off a bridge, on the same day that I was accepted into the school choir. Even though they never take anyone who is not in at least third year, but I auditioned and got all the high notes. 'Some Devil' I sang and if you don't get that right, then you can end up squeaking, but it was lovely, and I saw that Anna, that one in fourth year who is always going on as if she's been half discovered and is on her way to having made an album, even she was taken aback when I was auditioning and Weirauch said maybe we should just see how high I could go. So then he tried out the high notes with me. And then said, well, that's good, but can you sing low as well, and I could, and he said how extraordinary that is, that's what he said 'extraordinary', that I have such a wide range, and I don't know exactly what he said, but I can remember how Anna gave a jolt, and that I am 'extraordinary'. Me, a first year. So I wanted to go home and tell my parents. But nobody was there. So I waited and waited and waited and thought it was odd that Tom didn't come home. And then came the call.

And I know when I get there now, but maybe, I think, maybe they've been ringing to say, 'Jana, Tom has woken up! Tom is awake and is going to get better,' and then I'll go there and Mum and Dad will be laughing again at last and Tom will be sitting there, with his eyes open at last, and maybe he'll still have a bandage on, but there's a doctor there, looking into his file and nodding and smiling and slapping Tom on the back and Dad and Mum are shaking his hand, they're all so happy. But the ringing didn't sound like that.

Maybe they're just worried about me, so I should answer the phone quickly and calm their fears, that I'm OK, that nothing has happened to me, that I'm on my way home, and nothing like this will ever happen again, and even that would be all right, because it would be about me and not about Tom, but it didn't sound like that either.

And you can only take so many detours, at some stage your steps just won't go along with the messing, they just walk right in, where you don't want to go.

And there they are.

And they are not upstairs with Tom, they are standing outside, because you can't use the telephone upstairs, and I know as soon as I get there that I've gone wrong, that everything I do, that I say, it's all wrong, that I can't do anything right, and that nothing will ever be right again from today, from today the wrong time begins, or no, today it starts properly, WRONG TIME 2.0.

And where have you been, how come you're not answering your phone? What are you thinking of, could you not at least give a quick call, think of the worries we have, and we didn't know where to find you, your friends are all away (so I can spare myself that excuse), and Mum has me by the shoulders and is shaking me until she has shaken tears out of me.

I'm so afraid, I can't ask, I can't ask, I can't ask how things are with Tom, please, dear God, let everything be all right, please don't let them be like this because of Tom, please-please dear God or whoever decides these things, please-please don't let me have to ask, please, don't let them say, 'Jana, Tom is …' because I don't want to hear it, and Mum stops shaking and cries and cries and Dad turns around and I stand there and don't have to ask, and everything is pain and suffering and different, please, dear God, turn time back, don't let me be accepted into the choir, let me have come home earlier, and Tom is there and listens to me and says that I can try again next year, and that he thinks I have a great voice, dear God, let him not jump, please let him not fall. Please-please, Tom, be OK be alive and in one piece please-please-please make it different, because it hurts so much.

Louise

PEACE

And my parents were so delighted when there was a house there, a small one, and they rented it, it was near work so that they were always near the child, it was quiet and not a bad area and it was green.

And the house is in the shadow of the hospital and beside a graveyard and for that reason it is quiet and peaceful even though sometimes there are ambulance sirens and also bells ring; around the graveyard it is quiet, a noise-free zone. Though there are the bells.

And from the bedroom window of the little house you can climb onto the garage and from there it's just a little bit up again, such a small bit that you can make it even at eight years old and sit up there, with your knees knocking and your hands picking at the moss and look down. The trees are higher than the house but there are patches of light on the roof, which swim over the surface. And then if you squinch up your eyes a bit, then it looks a bit like what an eight-year-old imagines the seabed to be like, in the deep, dark with green spots. And you're a mermaid.

At seventeen you've got your eyes open wide, and the roof is a roof. And I haven't been here for ages, but the patches of light are still here.

And the bells are ringing.

There they go.

It rained last week, every day, everything was wet-wet-wet and it was all sticky, steamy.

The roof is black and warms up quickly. Last night took a rag and wiped the sky clean. Postcard weather.

If I look to the right I can see a little chapel. A little building from the seventies, dark wood, glass, flat. With enough seats and more chairs in a closet in case there aren't enough.

When the bells ring they walk slowly out of the chapel one behind the other to the graveyard. If you're eight years old and squinch up your eyes it's a swarm of fish that is going past. If you're seventeen it's people who are carrying someone to their grave. And you can't screw up your eyes because behind the coffin are three grown-ups and a girl, in fact you look more closely because the girl is further away, a little too far. I want to see her properly. Even though I know who it is I want to be sure, I can't make out if she is holding someone's hand, what she's looking at, if anyone has put an arm around her. That's why I strain my eyes, but it doesn't help.

There's a cheeky bird, far too loud, and I want to look towards him and put my finger to my lips. Or not. Because maybe that's exactly what the day needs, this loud bird.

And how much has happened, I think and also has not.

Nobody noticed about the car, and my gran came back and pressed a few notes into my hand, and I handed over Bonnie, and then there's all this thanks-thanks-thanks. And before that, Jonas came back because his money ran out, so that was the end of one job and the dog and then at the Corner Bakery the boss said that all the staff will be back from holidays on Monday so I am superfluous, that's how he put it, superfluous, the man doesn't beat about the bush.

So I have money, because Jonas has to pay me, whether he likes it or not, and the boss has finally paid me and I wasn't the only one keeping track of my hours but Angela too and she has the boss under her thumb.

And somehow that's how it all happened, so simple, I re-sat the theory examination a week later and didn't give it another thought, and passed.

And then the driving test itself and look, she has her driving licence and still can't drive, because Gran or one of my parents has to accompany me.

And everything is supposed to be fine and there is still some of the summer left.

But nothing really matters. And the thing that happened last year doesn't matter, the bells are ringing down there, and I can't see if Jana is walking on her own or if someone is holding her hand, just holding it at least, just a bit.

Jana

FUNERAL PARTY

It's as if someone suddenly flipped a switch. We're down from the cemetery and into the cars and then to the restaurant by the river, they have a room for us, tables and white tablecloths. And there is a smell of coffee, it's in pots on the tables, big pots, as if everyone is bloody tired, there is at least a litre of coffee each, and in between the coffeepots little bottles of lemonade and water. And there's cake, sandwiches, all waiting for us.

Am I allowed to be hungry?

Is the cake allowed to smell like that?

Everyone has been very softly spoken up to now, and we we're hardly there when it's off with jackets, because it is just too hot for jackets, and then they start to talk and get louder and Uncle Hannes has ordered a beer.

I have family. And lots of it. There are aunts and Granny Thesi, and another granny and grand-dad and great-aunts and cousins. Nobody dares to come over to me, I don't want to go over to them either. Luke has got his Nintendo out and is playing under the table because he's not supposed to, and the little ones are running outside. 'Would you not like to go out with them?' asks Granny.

Shrug. There's a playground outside, and the sand will still be wet. And in front of me is a piece of cake, smells perfect, there on the plate, all scrummy-looking and on top, only on top, sugar crystals glistening, and the cake is soft and smells of butter, real butter.

Yellow.

'Well, eat something first,' says Granny.

I look at the cake, there's a fork beside it, a little fork, which doesn't often have much to do, an elegant little Sunday-cake-fork. On Saturday. Cold to the touch, but I could pick it up, my fingers pick up the fork, the fork is above the cake, in the cake, how soft it is, it gives, like a cushion. 'Tell me, Jana,' says a man who's probably related to me, whom I do know, or maybe not, 'how old are you now?'

And because my mouth is full and I have to swallow and the cake is dry, even if it is buttery, and so the swallowing is a bit difficult, that's why Mum and Dad and Granny answer for me, because there are three empty mouths and one full, and Mum and Dad say, 'Twelve,' and Granny, 'Thirteen.'

And then they all look at each other, Granny with her eyebrows raised, Mum starts to smile but by now I have swallowed the cake and say, 'Thirteen.'

'No,' says Mum, and Dad says nothing.

'Yes,' I say.

And then she opens her mouth and Dad takes her hand (that hasn't happened for such a long time but now, there it is, Dad's hand on Mum's) and with her mouth still open, Mum looks at Dad and his eyes are wide.

Clinkety-clink, the penny drops.

Then Luke is standing in front of me saying: 'I-have-to-go-outside-want-to-come?' because Aunt Silke caught him playing.

I nod, I take the cake and Mum and Dad and Granny and the relation stay inside.

Through the restaurant, it's different there, and there are fish. Then out and the little ones are there on swings, shouting. Luke sits on the wall and gets his Nintendo out again.

I look towards the little ones, who are hitting each other and not being nice. Why do people always think children are nice to each other? And that it's only kids from trashy families who say things like: 'I have a gun and I'm going to shoot you dead.'

And dead.

I have no sunglasses and there's no shade here.

So I turn around, walk a few steps, and there's an opening in the wall, through, and walk on, a few metres, and nobody is calling me.

My jacket is still inside, over the back of a chair, and it stays there, because it's warm and near the jacket are people who ask where I'd like to go.

I go on, down the street, Luke still can't finish level seven, on I go and 'Aaaaaah! you're dead! I've killed you,' and on and on.

AND THE BAD THING

is that it goes on.

But the good thing is that it goes on. And that no story just comes to an end.

That you can always say,

and then,

and then you take a breath and it goes on.

Because the story isn't over yet.

AWAY

I'm away. Outside it's summer. Take me away out of the summer, take me out, subtract me.

I'm not here.

And my granny says I can come to her for a week before school starts. But I don't do that.

And my father says that he'll take me, if I like, and if it's just for a while, and that there's a room in his place that can be mine.

Or we could move away. Or go on holiday.

And my mother says it's lovely and warm out. And who has rung. And my mobile is done for. And no music.

Day and night, everything stays outside.

Leave me be.

And there's a ring at the door and somebody opens it, but my door stays closed and my cover is over me. It's dark, there's no air and not much room, I'm in here, no room for anyone else.

Sometimes I sleep, sometimes I'm awake.

Dark is good, at night I slip out, go into the kitchen, it's cool there underfoot, the fridge is there. I stand in front of it and cool my front, I close it again and look out the window, there's a street light that's on the blink. And at night I can go out the window, and I try a few steps, but even at night there are always people and the windows are lit and everyone is never asleep.

And everyone knows, everyone has read about it and has told everyone else about it, and they didn't even know his name, a hand to their mouth, and that he jumped, and weeks later he could die, was able to, managed it, that it is just a small thing that makes the body stop breathing, the heart stop beating, that it can be a little vein, or it's not exactly known.

And then the knocking, but I don't open, and if Mum is crying outside and if she says a thousand times that after all she has lost a child and that she is so sad and that she is sorry about my birthday, that I have to understand. And that I can't just stay in here all the time just because of that.

And I sit there and don't know what to say. It's not about birthdays any more. It's not about … I don't know. And I lie down again.

And then this card.

No stamp. No address, just JANA written on it.

Dear Josie
The jungle is green and you're not here. I drove on and I'm waiting for you at the equator, they have a fridge there, and they promise fresh biscuits. I'm doubtful but curious too. Haven't seen any new animals. Are you coming?
Love, Louana

And it's night or not but I have postcards. Blank ones.

Dear Comrade Louana
The war is still banging on. The air full of ashes and gunpowder. We wear masks, the children and the old people are being evacuated. We're drinking tinned food and eating stones. I'm in hiding.
Love, Josie

And out at night. Along the street with cap and sunglasses around corners and to her letter-box. No stamp, no address.

Dear Josie
No retreat, no surrender. The guerrillas in Omakoma have painted your face on their flags and want to sing battle songs. Do you still know the words? Can't get beyond 'the sail is made of liquourice/towards west-north-east/lace up gym-shoes against the rain/...'
Was that the pre-revolutionary version? Is there night there, where you are?
Your friend Louana

Louana.
Winter solstice in the Anti-Arctic. The days are getting wider now. You still can't tell hand from foot from belly-button. But that they still know there what I look like is a good thought. I have forgotten the words. But I'm working on it.
I have discovered hand-washing for myself. It is shocking hot for the time of year. The bears are selling sunglasses. One a day.
Josie

Ring-a-ring-a-josie
The sailors send their love, the wind is
slowly abating. The pirates are on union-
negotiated holidays, the sea is calm again.
Time to take swimming lessons. The ocean
is blue, the sky is blue and the helmsman is
quite green in the face.
Ahoy, Louana

P.S: Should I send supplies?

Louana.
Yes. We're short of everything. Please. Yes. Here: in
the eye of the storm. Everything still, but all around
it's roaring and raging. An anorak would be a start.
A bit of a one.
J.

Louise

CARE PACKAGE

Pack up your troubles in your old kit-bag.

I'm packing a parcel.

The war is over and Jana is in the occupied zone, I'm a candy bomber, I'm the Allies, I'm folding little parachutes, a box.

I pack a box and put in it:

- Decals of flowers and fairies, sparkling
- A stone, cold, smooth to the touch
- Marshmallows, because they are soft
- A pair of sunglasses, dark, but with a green frame, poisonous green, so green that you could not under any circumstances confuse it with another colour (something like hope)
- A baseball cap
- A photo of Bonnie and me
- A carton of chocolate milk (straw: striped)
- Socks. Yellow. One size fits all
- A night light. For the electric socket
- A postcard with elephants on it

Dear Josie.

It's time.
I'll knock when the coast is clear.
Then you can come out.

Love, Louana

Jana

TOUR GUIDE

I just can't sleep. I'm half asleep, half awake. At some time it's night, at some time Mum knocks again, but at some time she goes to bed too. She has to sleep.

When the parcel arrived, it was good, and smiling for the first time is weird. It's late now, it's so late that Mum is asleep, that Dad is sure to be asleep too, that there are no cars on the road any more, all is calm, one is bright. The shutter is up, I have the night-light on and it's good. It's quiet, I don't know what to make of the quiet. But no music, no.

And wait.

Listen. How silent it is here.

And then a rustling, then ears pricked and rustling, crrk-crrk, nearer, and a branch creaks.

'Josie,' comes a whispering, 'I'm going to knock.'

Then a little knock. Three times. And once again.

And then: 'You can come out now.'

I open the window.

'Aha! Are you ready?'

I nod. And climb out of the window.

When I am down and outside, there is the world and the

night and Louise-Louana.

'Cap?'

'Yeah.'

'Sunglasses?'

'Got them.'

'Supplies?'

I hold up the drink carton.

'The marshmallows?'

'All gone.'

'OK. Socks?'

We look down.

'On.'

She looks at me.

'What now?' I ask. 'Where to?'

'Wait and see. Me too.'

So we set off through the garden. We stop on the street.

'I've brought Bonnie,' she says.

And I do like dogs. And the dog likes me and has a name that I know, Bonnie wags and wags her tail at me. So I give her a little pat.

'Now what?' I ask.

'First stop: outdoors. Look, Josie, you are out of doors. So far so good?'

'Yeah,' I say, because it is OK.

'We'll walk a bit. Bonnie is not so fast. We have time. If you need anything, let me know. I hope you've been to the loo?'

'Yes,' I say.

'You're fibbing again,' she says with a smile.

And then we follow Bonnie.

And I am outside. Here is a dog, it is night. Here is the world, but it is dark and silent and a different kind of silent than in my room.

She doesn't say anything more, we just walk along quietly, just dog and footsteps in yellow socks, the night is a little darker with sunglasses, even with a full moon. It is warm enough and not hot, even with the cap, and it is always better to have a cap on than not.

And then I say: 'What were the decals for?'

'What?'

'Was there a reason for them?'

'They're decals. They're shiny. You can stick them on things or put them in a drawer. Decals have no purpose.'

'And now?'

'And now we're going to walk until something else occurs to us. But first we'll just walk.'

Louana

AND THEN?

And then they walk and they arrive. And sit down on the ground, here for example. It's not bad on the ground in summer, even in the city, you have trousers on, keep the dirt out, and it's not cold. There's something in front of us, we can look at it, at night it's sometimes enough just to sit and stare, overhead is the sky, it is black at night, and then Louana says that this here is outside. Here you are again, Josie.

'And then?' asks Josie.

'Then eventually the summer comes to an end.'

But maybe that is not enough. Maybe the two of them will walk on, because Josie is still the one who decides and says well-then, so-then, and so we keep going to wherever it is summer, and then it will never come to an end. And we don't need to go home, not even for supper, we can just keep on doing this for ever, even when your yellow socks are finally grey, then we'll just buy new ones. We'll be rich, because we have five good ideas and one of them works. We'll buy an island and breed dogs. And then we'll set up a ukulele band and we'll make music. We'll sing your brother a song and leave the smooth stone on his grave. And then we will be queens and wear crowns and people will write history about us. And then we'll lose our fear of bridges because they are not just for falling off. And we'll climb a mountain, save lives and take flying lessons. And then you ask if you are still allowed to be sad, and I say yes you're the one who decides, and you are allowed to be sad even if it is always summer and we have so much money that we can buy all the ice-cream in the world. And if we don't want any more ice-cream, then a sausage, and another one, with mustard but no roll. And then you say that you do want a roll. And I say OK. And then we will be superheroes without capes, but with masks.

Or maybe not. Maybe we'll wait until we get hungry and there is dew lying on us and we realise that we are tired. And then we'll eat something on the way home. And the sun rises, the night is over. 'Look, Josie, the night is over,' I say. 'Just look,' I say.

And that's as far as we've got.

ABOUT THE AUTHOR

Tamara Bach is one of Germany's leading authors for young adults.

Her first novel, *Marsmädchen* (available in English from the Canadian publisher Groundwood Books under the title *Girl from Mars*), won the Oldenburg Prize for Youth Literature and went on to win the overall German prize for youth literature in 2004. This book, *Wherever it is Summer* (originally entitled *Was vom Sommer übrig ist*) won the Catholic Children's and Youth Book Prize and the German–French Youth Literature Prize, both in 2013, and several of her other books have also won awards.

Tamara has lived in various parts of Germany and now lives and works in Berlin, where she completed her university studies. She loves to travel and has spent time in both Ireland and Britain. She speaks super English and was a huge help to the translator.

OTHER BOOKS IN TRANSLATION FROM LITTLE ISLAND BOOKS

Little Island knows that not everything that happens in the world happens in English, and that children deserve to hear other voices and see other points of view. That's why we like to publish books from other countries alongside our books by Irish authors.

Here is just a selection of our translated titles.

FOR TEENAGERS

No Heroes
by Anna Seidl
translated from German by Siobhán Parkinson
A gripping psychological study of how a group of teenage girls cope with and recover from the trauma, grief, loss and guilt left in the devastating wake of a school shooting

Thin Ice
by Mikael Engström
translated from Swedish by Susan Beard
The highly adventurous and moving story of how a young boy escapes his dysfunctional family and makes a new life in the Arctic north of Sweden

FOR OLDER CHILDREN

Bartolomé – The Infanta's Pet
by Rachel van Kooij
translated from German by Siobhán Parkinson
The story of how a severely disabled boy copes with life in the
court of Philip IV in 17th-century Spain

The History Mystery
by Ana Maria Machado
translated from Brazilian Portuguese by Luisa Baeta
A group of boys and girls unravel clues from the past and learn
about the importance of books and history

Fennymore and the Brumella
by Kirsten Reinhardt
illustrated by David Roberts
translated from German by Siobhán Parkinson
A zany voyage of discovery to find Fennymore's missing parents

FOR YOUNGER CHILDREN

The Wizardling
by Binette Schroeder
Gorgeous picturebook with a fairy-tale atmosphere

Cow Belle Beauty Queen
by Leena Parkkinen
illustrated by Katja Wehner
translated by Ruth Urbom
A super-mad story of a cow with beauty-queen aspirations

SEE WWW.LITTLEISLAND.IE/INTERNATIONAL-BOOKS FOR MORE